DI   W   AB
7/17   7/18 9/19

To renew this book, phone 0845 1202811 or visit
our website at www.libcat.oxfordshire.gov.uk
(for both options you will need your library PIN
number available from your library),
or contact any Oxfordshire library

OXFORDSHIRE
COUNTY COUNCIL

L017-64 (01/13)

BLACK BARGAIN

Joan Wentworth, a newly qualified nurse, nearly faints from the ether whilst assisting the famous surgeon, Dr. Lancaster, and is promptly suspended from her job. That evening, when she pleads with him to reinstate her, she is surprised to be invited to work at his hospice that serves the poor hill people of Pennsylvania. Joan accepts; but on her arrival at the remote institute, she finds herself plunged into an atmosphere of menace and mystery. No one there seems to be normal — not least Dr. Lancaster himself when he visits . . .

VICTOR ROUSSEAU

◆

BLACK BARGAIN

Complete and Unabridged

LINFORD
Leicester

First published in Great Britain

First Linford Edition
published 2017

A catalogue record for this book is available
from the British Library.

ISBN 978–1–4448–3311–9

Published by
F. A. Thorpe (Publishing)
Anstey, Leicestershire
Set by Words & Graphics Ltd.
Anstey, Leicestershire
Printed and bound in Great Britain by
T. J. International Ltd., Padstow, Cornwall
This book is printed on acid-free paper

1

Joan Is Suspended

'I let him see I wouldn't stand for any language like that, and I reckon he understood, even if I didn't have to say much,' remarked the dark-haired woman to Joan Wentworth. 'It doesn't seem to have occurred to Dr. Lancaster yet that a nurse is a human being under her uniform. If he'd treat us half as nicely as he treats some of his lady friends ... ' she added in a suggestive tone that changed into the accentuation of ordinary speech under Joan's discouraging look. 'I've seen him driving them round town nights in his auto, and I've never seen the same one twice. I guess he takes it out on us when they've been mean to him.'

Joan did not answer her. She was watching the head surgeon as he came into the operating theater. At his entrance the general buzz of conversation ceased as if the outpouring of words had been cut off with a knife. The students on the benches settled themselves in their places and craned their heads forward intently. The two assistant surgeons, Ivers and MacPherson, assumed attitudes of constraint, for everybody was constrained in Lancaster's presence. The orderly, who had been peering through the crack of the swinging door into the anesthetic room, where the head nurse was holding the patient's wrist and watching the face beneath the mask intently, straightened himself and stood up in military fashion.

Only the visiting doctors seemed at their ease as they advanced to shake hands with John Lancaster. They had come from several neighboring cities, drawn by the news that Lancaster was to perform his famous operation of arterial excision, which was just then the subject of discussion in the medical press. Plenty of surgeons had tried to remove a section of one of the larger blood vessels, but only Lancaster had succeeded in bringing down the mortality to fifteen percent.

Lancaster was something of a mystery both to his colleagues and to the nursing staff. The Lancaster Fund supported the

Southern Hospital, and John Lancaster was firmly established at the head of the institution. The board of guardians, which existed according to the terms laid down in his father's will, had apparently only an advisory capacity, and it was supple and plastic in Lancaster's hands. And John Lancaster was more feared and admired than any doctor in the country.

Feared by most for his tyranny, admired by a very few on account of his extraordinary skill, he seemed to have a dual personality. The man whose fast life was the scandal of the conservative little southern seaport, who was ostracized by the better families, whose infrequent appearances in the hospital were usually the occasion for injustice, storms, and dismissals, changed in the operating theater into a man whose gentleness and humility and skill made him adored for the time by all who came into contact with him. But it was only rarely that a case occurred that required his attention.

On such occasions his manner was in itself remarkable. He would slip stealthily into his private room, dress there, and emerge masked like a mummy to perform

3

his miracle almost in silence, and afterward to make his escape in a way suggestive of his having performed some shameful action.

So much Joan Wentworth had heard. Naturally she watched his entrance on this her first day of surgical work with absorbed interest unshaken by the dark-haired woman's scandalous revelations. But Lancaster came in unmasked, and Joan could discern nothing humble or secretive in the self-satisfied face or the brisk manner in which he greeted the visiting surgeons.

He looked a man of seven or eight and thirty, and he bore his years heavily. The eyes were lined and a little sunken; and the features, which Joan had seen only a few times during her eighteen months of work at the hospital, exercised, as they had always done, a rather repellent effect. The face was eminently cruel and hard. Nevertheless the man obviously dominated the assembly.

He dominated her. She was much more afraid of some nervous lapse in Lancaster's presence than of seeing the use of the knife. The hissing of the steam tank; the nervous movements of the spectators upon the benches, whose heads seemed to swing with a uniform and rhythmical motion; and the deepening sense of constraint acted upon her with a sort of hypnotic effect not lessened by Lancaster's decisive manner.

She pulled the tray of instruments out of the boiling water and set it down upon the table by the side of the dichloride solution. Lancaster, who had been pulling on his rubber gloves, came to her side, and plunged both hands into the antiseptic fluid. There was a look of self-conscious satisfaction upon his face, and Joan thought that every gesture and each movement was designed to impress the visitors.

Presently she became sure of it. The man was acting. A feeling of disgust came over her.

Lancaster cast a quick glance at Joan. 'New nurse?' he asked.

'My first morning of surgical work, Dr. Lancaster,' she answered.

He grunted in a contemptuous sort of way. Joan flushed to the hair. He turned to the other woman. 'You there!' he shouted. 'Look alive with those sponges!' And he cast a quick glance toward the visitors, as if to see whether they appreciated his harshness.

5

A look of chagrin came over the dark-haired woman's face, but she ran to obey and dropped the wet sponges into the dichloride with shaking fingers. At the same moment the swing door opened and the stretcher with the patient appeared, wheeled by the orderly. Behind it walked the head nurse, still maintaining her crouching attitude as she moved.

The stretcher stopped inside the theater, and the head nurse and orderly lifted the man who lay upon it on the glass table. He mumbled and tried to raise himself. The nurse put her hands about his shoulders, pressing them down, while the orderly held the body, protesting against the indignity about to be offered to it, to which it had emphatically not consented, whatever arrangement had been decreed by the brain.

Lancaster's harsh voice boomed through the theater: 'That's no way to bring a patient here, Miss Symons! Deep anesthesia!'

The head nurse lifted her face for an instant. 'There's a history of nephritis, Dr. Lancaster,' she said. 'The pulse is one-fifty, and Dr. MacPherson said — '

'Who's running this business?' shouted

Lancaster, striding toward her; and Joan was sure that he looked out of the corner of his eye toward the visitors.

He snatched the green ether bottle out of the nurse's hand and poured a quantity of the fluid upon the mask. The struggles ceased, the man sighed deeply, and his limbs relaxed. The nauseating stench of the ether fumes made Joan's head reel. It seemed to fill the theater. Miss Symons, flushing but displaying no resentment, took the bottle from Lancaster's hand and resumed her position, holding the patient's wrist and peering into his face, the green bottle upraised.

Lancaster went back to the foot of the table and the visiting surgeons clustered about him. Joan had never found him so detestable as at that moment.

The woman who was in charge of the sponges whispered bitterly to her: 'He doesn't know how to treat a woman — nor a lady. He isn't our kind. My, he must have been on a terrible racket last night! He can't keep up that gait much longer unless he gives up his work here.'

Joan ignored her; she had concentrated

all her attention upon Lancaster's probable demands and was resolved not to be found wanting. It was said that Lancaster was absolutely merciless, and had ruined many a woman's career by refusing to allow her to complete her graduating course. He was tyrannical, overlooked nothing, and never appreciated good work.

Rumor went that when a certain nurse had once handed him benzine instead of alcohol, he had taken her by the shoulders and run her bodily out of the hospital, forbidding her to show her face there again.

'He can't last long if he leads that sort of life,' the dark-haired woman repeated. 'You'd think he'd be old enough to have learned how to pretend to be a gentleman, even if he isn't one.'

Joan shook her off mentally as one chases away a persistent fly. For the tenth time she counted the instruments in the tray. Lancaster picked up a scalpel, and MacPherson and Ivers took up their positions, one on either side of him. The operation was beginning.

The visiting surgeons watched, with an occasional whispered remark. The assistants already were snapping the little forceps upon the ends of the divided arteries. Lancaster issued his commands from time to time, without looking back.

'Sponges!'

'One — two,' whispered the dark-haired woman. 'Three — four — five — '

'Bistoury. Scissors. Dilator. Number four Simms.'

Joan never faltered. She felt easier in her mind; her quick hands found the instruments in the tray the moment Lancaster demanded them.

Meanwhile, the dark-haired woman never ceased counting the sponges: 'Six — seven — eight — nine — '

Suddenly Lancaster stopped, wheeled, and turned fiercely upon her. 'For God's sake, stop that chatter!' he cried.

The woman let a sponge fall, snatched it up, and shot an apprehensive glance at him. Joan saw that she was losing her nerve in spite of her brave talk of a few minutes before. She redoubled her eagerness, but Lancaster's treatment of her companion was now beginning to frighten her. It was the critical time of a very dangerous and difficult process. She tried to pull herself together.

Yet without looking up, she realized that a sense of general apprehension had stolen through the operating theater. The nurse at the head of the table, looking like a veiled vestal, had not shifted her position since the beginning of the operation, except that from time to time her hand shifted slightly as she let one or two drops of ether fall upon the mask.

MacPherson and Ivers stirred busily, their heads bent level with their chief's as they moved to and fro at their work. The patient began to mutter again. Then a hand, upraised in weak protest, struck a clamp from Ivers's fingers. It rattled upon the floor.

'Keep him quiet, Miss Symons, confound you!' shouted Lancaster.

'Dr. Lancaster, the pulse — ' she began. But, after a quick glance at the head surgeon, she shrugged her shoulders, tilted the bottle, and deliberately poured out nearly all the ether remaining in it. The renewed stench of the anesthetic filled the room.

Joan saw the benches swing, and the

craning faces seemed to become multiplied. Lancaster and the two assistants, the visiting surgeons, were tiny gnomes an immense distance away, surrounding a tiny table on which a doll-like figure lay extended. Joan tried to bring them back into focus, but could not; and, what was worse, she felt that she had lost the nurse's sense of divining the surgeon's requirements before he gave expression to them.

Something was wrong; and although nothing had been said, even the students on the top row of benches furthest from the table were aware of it. The assistant doctors appeared as busy as over, and yet they seemed at a loss, and once or twice looked up at Lancaster as if his technique was puzzling them.

Joan saw two of the visiting surgeons exchange brief glances, one with inquiry and the other, answering, with uplifted eyebrows. Once Lancaster stopped; then he resumed his work, stopped again, and stood staring at his work. Then he wheeled round upon Joan, the upper part of his body seeming to move upon a pivot while his lower limbs remained stationary.

'That scalpel — quick!' he cried.

Joan started and stretched out her hands toward the tray, which gleamed far off elusively through a black cloud.

'The one I handed you. Don't stare at me like a fool!'

Joan bent over the tray, putting out one hand to the table to support herself. She was conscious that everything was suspended and that everyone was watching her. She sensed a little triumph and a little malice in the attitude of the dark-haired woman.

In the interminable interval, she heard the patient's gasping sighs, as if he were breathing the last wisps of life away.

She fingered the instruments in the tray feebly and nervelessly, and her hands seemed numb and useless. Her fingers closed on something and brought it out. Then Lancaster's hand closed over hers, tore it away, and flung it back with a splash. Joan's hand dropped to her side, paralyzed by the painful pressure. The next instant Lancaster had the scalpel and whirled swiftly back toward the table, upsetting the dichloride, which lapped over the patient's feet.

'Seventeen — eighteen,' the dark-haired woman was whispering under her breath.

The moments went by like hours. At last Joan became aware, through the sudden unraveling of the suspense, that the crux of the operation was over. Her head grew clear again. She saw the assistant surgeons unfastening the artery clamps. Ivers had his needle and the sutures in his hand; MacPherson was closing the wound. The dark-haired woman was still counting her sponges.

The head nurse rose to her feet, not looking at the patient. Joan realized that she was crying, and her strong, epicene face looked grotesque in grief. The orderly came up and together they placed the patient on the stretcher. And suddenly Joan knew that the man was dead.

As the stretcher was wheeled out of the theater, Lancaster turned toward his visitors. 'A very successful piece of work,' he said. 'It's a pity the poor follow will never know how much I have done for him.'

Joan felt the visiting surgeons' disgust at the execrable jest. Lancaster seemed to sense it, too.

'Unfortunately,' he continued, 'the best of surgeons is not proof against the stupidity of a nurse.' And he turned upon Joan fiercely. 'What is your name?' he demanded.

'Miss Wentworth, Dr. Lancaster.'

'Well, you're no use here. You're wasting your time. You've killed a man this morning,' he bellowed. 'If I can't have women about me with rational heads on their shoulders, I'll get a gang of men. Get out and earn your living as a stenographer or saleslady. That's all your talents are fit for, Miss Wentworth!'

Joan looked at him in amazement. At his first words, at his tone, she had felt the shock of anger in her heart gather itself and leap to meet his own. But his rage frightened her, her head ached, and she was sick from the fumes which still penetrated the theater. She tried to answer him, but could not utter a word and broke into tears instead, sobbing in complete nervous abandonment.

Lancaster turned from her with a wry face. 'Well, gentlemen,' he said with an affectation of joviality, 'better luck next time. I'm sorry the operation was not successful; but, after all, the patient's life is not the principal thing. The method was correct, you see, but I did not reckon on an incompetent assistant.'

'Put the blame on the anesthetic, Dr. Lancaster,' said a white-bearded surgeon with chivalrous intent. 'With a nephritis history, an operation's useless. Better let them die peacefully.'

'I did not quite grasp the technical innovation you spoke of, Dr. Lancaster,' said another. 'To my mind it was the original Leonard operation, except that — '

'Why did you divide the arterial coats below the site of the aneurism?' queried a third.

Lancaster led them from the theater, expostulating and explaining. The dark-haired woman lingered with the sponges. The assistant surgeons had already hurriedly gone out. Joan put her tray away. She was still unable to control her sobs.

Suddenly Lancaster reappeared, furious after the cross-examination to which he had been subjected. He came straight toward Joan with a face of malice.

Unconscious of her pitiful aspect as

a child might have been, she raised her streaming face and looked at him. 'You had no right to speak to me like that, whatever I did,' she said.

'Whatever you did? Whatever you failed to do! What do you think you're here for?' he stormed.

He glared at her, turned away, hesitated, and then came back. 'That's just the way with you women,' he cried. 'You lost that case for me. And now you're thinking about your dignity. You shouldn't have taken a nurse's vocation. You women don't know what you can do and what you can't till you find yourselves in a post of responsibility, and then you fall down. What made you take up nursing, anyway? Thought our style of caps becoming, I suppose.'

'I've done my best to qualify. I've never been blamed before.'

'Well, you've made a big mistake,' said Lancaster. 'That's all. A very big mistake,' he added, emphasizing each word with a nod. 'And my work and patients' lives are too important to allow mistakes to happen. You're too pretty to be a nurse, anyway,' he added in a lower tone.

'You don't need to tell me that, Dr. Lancaster!' cried Joan furiously.

He made a gesture of mock despair. 'That's right, get on your high horse again!' he said. 'Just remember that I'm the Head of the Southern Hospital, and what I say goes, that's all.' He swung upon his heel and went out of the room, leaving Joan gripping the table fiercely in her humiliation.

The dark-haired woman, who had been fussing in a corner, came up to her. 'He's a beast!' she exclaimed passionately. 'He hates women — decent women. My! If he'd dared to speak that way to me, I'd have told him what I thought of him, right in the middle of the operation. I don't care for anybody when my temper's up. I could tell you a few things I've heard about him if I were minded to. Do you know he went on a five-year spree once?'

'I don't care what he did!' cried Joan passionately.

'Well, I guess you could make it your business to know,' answered the other. 'A woman's got to fight her way the same as a man. He threw his job away and just vanished for five years, drinking and living with

17

tramps, and then had the nerve to come back as if nothing had happened. I got it from a woman who used to be friendly with him. He's — ' She broke off abruptly as the orderly appeared with his rubber broom and bucket. Then: 'What are you going to do about it?' she inquired in a low voice. 'I reckon you don't want to forfeit your diploma any more than the rest of us. Listen! You go and see him.'

'Never!' said Joan.

'Don't be a fool, Miss Wentworth! You go and see him at his house. It's what anyone would do in your place. Fool him by making him think he can do what he likes with you; play with him and hold him off by hook or crook until you've graduated, and then laugh at him. I'd do it if I had to. My! If you heard some of the stories that are going round ... '

The head nurse beckoned at the door. 'The superintendent wants to see you at once, Miss Wentworth,' she said. 'You're to go right into her office.'

She looked at Joan resentfully. Her face was quite composed again, but her eyes were reddened. She knew that Lancaster had been at fault, but she had seen Joan's blunder, too. Miss Symons was one of those women who could acquire the faculty of a man's strength without losing the qualities of her own sex. She was a tower of strength toward weakness, but she had no pity for a lapse of duty.

Joan walked the dreary length of the corridor to the superintendent's room. The white-haired woman was seated at her desk, pretending to be making up her accounts and composing herself for the interview.

'Miss Wentworth!' she began, turning round in her chair as Joan appeared at the door. 'You have made Dr. Lancaster very angry. He says you're totally inefficient. What was it that happened this morning?'

'The ether made me faint and I couldn't see the instruments for a moment, and Dr. Lancaster happened to want a scalpel quickly,' answered Joan.

'Well, it's a great pity,' said the other, 'because it was your first day. We had to get somebody to take Miss Martin's place, and I selected you because I relied on you particularly. Anyway, you are suspended.'

Joan looked at her, stupefied. Though she

had nerved herself for this, she realized at that moment that she had never expected the decision.

'You mean that I am to leave the hospital and lose my diploma?' she asked.

'I don't know yet,' answered the superintendent evasively. 'I suppose Dr. Lancaster will decide that later, after he's laid the matter before the board at the next meeting and looked over your record. As you know, he doesn't usually change his mind. And what he says goes with the board. Anyway, Miss Wentworth, you may as well take a holiday for a week or so until you hear from us.'

She turned back to her books, while Joan, after looking at her for a moment in silence, turned and went into the corridor. She made her way toward the hospital entrance. And the great wooden arch, through which she had passed hundreds of times without noticing it, suddenly became vivid with detail; the hospital, which had been a part of her unconscious life, looked strange and new to her.

Joan had a room in a nurses' boarding house a few minutes' walk away. The nurses' building had burned down two years previously, and the funds of the institution had not enabled it to complete the reconstruction of the edifice.

She walked mechanically homeward, hardly even yet realizing the magnitude of the blow which had befallen her. The events of the morning were already becoming blurred and unreal.

Avonmouth lay almost deserted in the noontide glare. The shuttered houses, gay with striped awnings, looked down on the white, dusty streets. The little park that contained the confederate monument was bright with geraniums, but the grass was parched and withered, and the feeble efforts of an automatic sprinkler seemed almost instantly absorbed by the thirsty ground.

Joan made her way toward an overhanging tree, brushed away a prickly caterpillar from a seat beneath it, and sat down. She looked across the park at the red blotch made by the hospital against the water oaks. She was trying to estimate the magnitude of the catastrophe that had happened to her, to free herself from the stupefied wonder and passionate resentment that held her.

Two hours before, life had seemed reasonably bright; now its entire course was changed. She did not doubt that the superintendent had been trying to soften the news of her dismissal.

Her mind ran back to the beginning of all things for her — her father's death. That had happened ten years before; and the mortgage on the estate, ruined after the war, had grown like a spreading sore, eating away field after field, until it swallowed everything except nine hundred dollars. After the enforced sale, Mrs. Wentworth and her daughter had gone to Avonmouth for the sole reason that the mother remembered a wealthy godmother there, distantly related, whose activities she hoped to enlist on behalf of her daughter. It was characteristic of her that she should not have known the woman had died six years previously.

Still, Avonmouth was the nearest large town in which a woman, flung on the world untrained, might hope to support two people. Joan had long before wanted to be a nurse. She decided to attempt to enter a hospital, but her mother's terminal illness had kept her nursing her at home. Six months after their arrival, Mrs. Wentworth died. What remained of their nine hundred dollars after the doctor's and funeral expenses had been paid would suffice for Joan's merest needs until she had graduated from the Southern Hospital. But the physician who attended Mrs. Wentworth in her illness had secured Joan a position as a probationer, and Joan was as happy as she could expect to be. Since that date he had moved away, and she was altogether alone.

At home they had known hardly anyone. Their friends had scattered to the north and west, and their letters had long since ceased. Prosperity, stalking through the nation, had left a little ridge of poverty between the swaths of its progress through the foothills of the back country.

In Avonmouth Mrs. Wentworth's illness, and afterward the hospital work, had kept Joan both from making friends and from the realization of her need of them. Her whole mind was set upon obtaining that diploma, which would mean an assured living; and before her eyes was ever the spectacle of such poverty as she had known at home among others and had been approaching her mother. After she graduated, perhaps life might begin to unfold before her eyes. But even this she realized only vaguely; she lived altogether in the moment.

In the town of forty thousand inhabitants, Joan was as isolated as she had been in the latter years at home. Her life was as unsophisticated and as simple, and she was so unacquainted with the conditions and circumstances of existence that her dismissal seemed to her an irreparable disaster.

She had won good opinions, she had been praised, and it seemed monstrous that her faintness at a critical moment should have ruined her whole life prospects. What made the tragedy the less tolerable was the added mixture of the farcical. There was a simple and absurd explanation: Mrs. Webb's cook, Amanda, had quarreled with her mistress that morning, and Joan had had to go to the hospital without her breakfast.

2

Joan Is Given a Mysterious Mission

Joan got up and walked slowly homeward without having solved her problem. Inside the boarding house the air was like a furnace, and the smell of cooking was triumphant and dominant, as if in self-assertion after its earlier suppression. Inside the kitchen, seen through the open door, was Amanda returned, penitent, greasy, tear-stained, and yet radiant; and Mrs. Webb was standing near her with that happy expression which women cherish when a household quarrel has been made up and the domestic problem put back for later consideration.

'Here's Amanda again!' the landlady called to Joan. 'My dear, the idea of your running away without your breakfast this morning —! Now you sit right down and have your lunch, Miss Wentworth.'

Joan was not hungry, but it was impossible to oppose the resolute insistence of

Mrs. Webb, backed by the penitent cook, whose face, as she flitted from the kitchen to the dining room, radiated remorse and good intentions.

'One can't get along without the proper food at the proper time,' said Mrs. Webb as she set down the steaming dishes. 'But I call it real sensible of you to have come home early. Some people wouldn't have thought of that.'

Joan choked suddenly, and Mrs. Webb perceived her distress. She bent over her and placed a kitchen-roughened hand upon her shoulder. 'My dear, what is it? What's the matter? Something gone wrong at that old hospital?' she asked. 'Tell me now, honey.'

'It isn't anything, Mrs. Webb,' said Joan, striving valiantly to keep back her tears. 'I've been — I'm discharged.'

Mrs. Webb withdrew her hand and placed it upon one hip, bringing the other into corresponding position. She glared at Joan as the convenient focus for her indignation. 'I never heard of such a thing!' she cried. 'Who's dared to discharge you, Miss Wentworth? Why, it was only yesterday

Miss Gray was saying you were the only nurse in the hospital that attended to her work instead of trying to make dates with the doctors! I've had the nurses two years now, Miss Wentworth, and they ain't a snap better than the salesladies I used to keep; a pack of featherheads! If some of them had been discharged, it would serve them right. But not you, my dear. It's that old Dr. Lancaster!'

'It was, and I think he was right. I felt faint from the smell of ether —'

'Of course you did!' cried Miss Webb. 'I always knew the day would come when you would. Those smells make my head go round and round whenever I take the short cut that side of the park. I always said you weren't cut out for that sort of work. It's all right for them women that's made for it, but what you need is to marry some good man who can take care of you, not to go nursing a lot of dock hands and seeing people's insides opened up. It's my belief that when the Lord put our insides in and our outsides out, he meant them to stay there,' snorted Mrs. Webb.

'Well,' said Joan wearily, 'it's ended now.

And I don't know what I'm going to do.'

'But I say it isn't ended!' cried Mrs. Webb, concentrating all her indignation against Lancaster in a venomous glare. 'It's only just begun. If that old doctor dares to discharge you, I'm going to tell everything I know about him. Miss Wentworth, that man's no more fit to be the head of a hospital with ladies under him than he's fit to fly. What is he? Nothing but a fast-liver and a common drunkard. To think of a man like that, who went about with a gang of common tramps for years, Miss Wentworth, just breaking away from his job and hoboing it up and down the country — and then coming back and getting his job again and doing as he does! And that I say is common knowledge. Five years after the hospital had seen the last of him, in he walks, as bold as brass, and puts the head doctor out, and says the hospital's his and he's going to run it again. And him being in charge of the nurses — him that runs round in his auto with every pack of cheap actresses that come to Avonmouth! I know what they are! I haven't been in the boarding-house business twenty years for nothing!'

Mrs. Webb was becoming incoherent. Joan acceded in stopping the flow of vilification at last, mainly because Mrs. Webb had exhausted it.

'Now I tell you what you're going to do, my dear,' she said. 'You're going straight to that old Lancaster's house and you're going to ask for your place back. And you're going to get it, too.'

'Mrs. Webb, how can I do that?'

'How can you do it? Why, you can manage him all right, my dear. Yes, I guess it's going to be all right. I suppose he lost his temper. When a man leads the sort of life he does, he hasn't much good humor left the morning after. I know about that. You just go to him and act as if you didn't care much, and let him think you look on him as just the —'

'Please, Mrs. Webb!' expostulated Joan; and as she spoke there came back into her mind vividly the sinister advice of the dark-haired woman.

'You've only got to let him see your face, my dear,' continued the landlady. 'You see, it's this way: When he's in the hospital he's thinking about his work. A nurse is just a nurse to him then. But after his work is over, she's different. Now don't tell me you can't make that man do anything you want him to, because I know better.'

Joan crimsoned. 'I couldn't think of such a thing,' she protested.

'And why not?' inquired the other. 'If you've got good looks, ain't you going to use them? It isn't as if I was asking you to do anything wrong, is it? You'd be a precious fool if you didn't. Any woman can twist a man round her finger, especially if she looks weepy.'

Joan looked at Mrs. Webb in great distress. She rose, but the landlady followed her toward the door.

'You see, my dear,' she went on, 'if you were given that sort of face by the Almighty, why shouldn't you use it to get plain, common justice done you? It's your job that's at stake, and you all alone in the world. All you've got to do is to make him forget that he's dealing with a nurse. Why, doesn't every man have his pull somewhere? Even Mr. Webb, who never amounted to a snap, had his pull — he got me the street-department clerks as boarders. And where's your pull, outside your looks? There isn't anybody would think twice about it. Didn't Amanda do it this morning, coming to me with her big, honest face, and looking at me so that I had to take her back, as I was glad enough to do? You go straight and see that old Lancaster and try it, that's all.'

A nurse passed the window and came up the steps.

'Mrs. Webb, you won't say a word about what I've told you to the others, please?' asked Joan.

Without waiting for a reply, she flew upstairs and, flinging herself down on her bed, stared out dismally toward the monument. The catastrophe had swept her little unsheltered world away. She realized now that she was as much a stranger in Avonmouth as when she arrived, a woman of twenty, with her mother, two years before. The sense of her loneliness swept over her like a black cloud, appalling her. She was cut off from life, and utterly helpless outside the medium in which she had lived.

Because she felt this sense of homelessness, her outraged pride began to vanish before the terrors that her imagination conjured up. Starvation, the ultimate terror of her childish days on the estate which, like a living thing, had gnawed into her mother's nine hundred dollars, seemed incredibly real and near. So Mrs. Webb's solution, not in its scope of intrigue but in its essentials, became the commonplace resolution of her difficulty. She must ask for her position back! She must face Lancaster in his home, humble her pride, and bow to him. But she watched the sun decline and the shadows lengthen, for a time she could not bring herself to her task.

What strengthened her at last was the realization that her status must be settled before she faced the day-nurses coming home off duty. She slipped on her cloak and went out of the house softly, glad to escape the landlady's attentions. It was near sunset; the birds were singing in the park, which was cool after the day. Joan went hastily toward Lancaster's house.

She had passed it almost daily, on her journeys to and from the hospital. It was an ordinary brick house in a row block at the north end of the park, and commonplace enough; but now, to her excited eyes, it seemed to reflect the grim personality of its owner in the staring windows, with the shining doorknobs and name plate of brass. Her heart was beating with panic, and it was with difficulty that she contrived to press the bell and remain until the door was opened.

An attendant confronted her — a sullen, undersized man with square shoulders who scowled at her as he stood blocking the passage. A shaft from the setting sun breaking from behind a cloud illuminated the entire length of the street, making the interior gloom almost darkness.

'Dr. Lancaster?' asked Joan.

'He doesn't see patients after six,' answered the man.

'I must see him. I'm not here as a patient! It's important,' she faltered.

'Well. I'll find out if he can see you,' the fellow grumbled.

He had not recognized Joan's uniform beneath the cloak. She went into the waiting room. There the sense of the terror which made that place its domain — the accumulated fears of all who had ever waited there for the approaching verdict — seemed to leap out at her. The torn magazines upon the table were a mockery; the ticking of the clock the register of eternity.

Then Joan heard Lancaster's voice in the next room, which was divided from the waiting room by folded doors. It was audible as a bass rumble, emerging occasionally into a distinguishable word. Lancaster was talking with somebody, and he was growing angry. That was an ill omen of what was to come!

Joan braced her nerves. She was anything but a coward, and having made up her mind, she intended to carry the scheme through.

Suddenly Lancaster's voice was raised in violent altercation. 'A nice mess you've made of everything!' he cried. 'I've tolerated you too long. I've been a fool, but I've finished with you now. Go back where you came from!'

Another voice spoke in indistinct tones. It was that of a man, and it was almost abject in contrast with Lancaster's violence.

'I've finished with you, I tell you!' cried Lancaster. 'I've borne this burden long enough. You can get out of my house. You can get out of my life.'

'I've borne it long enough, too,' replied the other doggedly. 'Who started it? Who made the first proposal?'

'I did, out of kindness to you. And how have you repaid me?'

'By placing myself, soul and body, at your service,' retorted the second man, aroused into some show of spirit.

'Who picked you out of the gutter and set you on your feet?' rejoined the doctor. 'Answer me that! You can't! You know you can't! Where would you be today if it were not for me?'

The second man said something in a low voice.

'Myers? A lot I care about that!' retorted Lancaster. 'I tell you — what's that?' The attendant was speaking at the door. Joan recognized his rasping voice.

'No! No!' cried Lancaster violently. 'I see nobody. Why can't these women come during my hours? Aren't they posted plainly enough upon the card in my window? Tell her — what? Important? Well, let her wait, then, until I get ready to see her.'

The man's steps died away along the

rear end of the passage. Joan heard the two men talking again. Then the sounds ceased. She heard the floor in the adjoining room creak beneath a quick tread. Lancaster was coming in. Her fear gave her resolution. She left the waiting room and went into the hall.

It was hung with little pictures of a uniform size, each exactly like its neighbor. It came into Joan's mind, even during her few hasty steps, that this was essentially a man's house. A woman would have arranged things differently, have given the place personality, have made her presence felt somehow, even in the decoration of this dark passage. The atmosphere was that of an institution, not of a home.

Then she was standing with caught breath at the door of the consulting room, which was a little ajar, as if the catch had become unfastened. She knocked, opened it, and went in.

She found herself in a large, lighter room, with the same sense of an institution, though it was well furnished. She saw the white enameled table, the glass case full of instruments, the empty court outside; then John Lancaster himself, alone, standing with bent head behind a chair, on which he was leaning.

As Joan entered, an inner door began to open. Joan knew that the man with whom Lancaster had been quarrelling was inside a room behind it. She dreaded his appearance, but suddenly the door closed. She looked at Lancaster again. It was still quite light within the consulting room, but Lancaster, standing with his back to the window, was in silhouette, so that Joan could not see his face clearly.

'Well, madam?' he asked, raising his head.

'I came to speak to you about this morning,' began Joan hurriedly. 'It means — '

He indicated a chair. He was gazing at her with some embarrassment — Joan thought because of the scene in which he had just participated.

'Tell me the trouble,' he began as she seated herself, drawing up his own chair toward hers.

Now Joan could see his face, and to her astonishment, it did not bear the expression of the smirking bully whom she had seen that morning, nor yet of the man who had addressed another man in such terms as one might use to a slave. It was not an unkindly face. And it was unmistakably that of a sick man.

For a moment she remembered the stories told of his behavior in the operating theater; of the gentleness that seemed to transform the man, as if he possessed a dual personality. Then she was recalled to herself by Lancaster's repetition of his remark.

Joan rose up hastily. She realized that the doctor had mistaken her for a patient. Her face meant nothing to him, any more than her distress of the day had affected him. With a nervous movement she unfastened her cloak, disclosing her uniform.

'I am Miss Wentworth,' she explained, treading out her pride once more. 'I came to ask if you won't reconsider your decision to suspend me. My work means everything to me. It is my life, my vocation. I always wanted to be a nurse. I felt that it was my task to help to alleviate suffering. Won't you give me another opportunity?'

She spoke with her hands unconsciously clasped before her; the recollection of her earlier hopes, the thought of their frustration, brought a quiver into her voice. When she stopped, she saw that Lancaster was looking at her with obvious interest.

'Tell me about this morning,' he said quietly.

'I had had to come away without breakfast, and the fumes of the ether made me feel faint. I was nearly unconscious when you asked me for the scalpel, and I couldn't see the tray. Indeed, it was not the operation that made me faint. I have never been reprimanded before. The superintendent had told me several times that the hospital appreciated my work. So I hoped you would be willing to overlook my blunder and let me graduate.'

Lancaster looked at her with a singular expression that seemed to mask his thoughts. She could not tell how her plea had impressed him. When he spoke, she was dumfounded by the harshness and casualness of his tone.

'Why have you come to my house about this?' he asked. 'This is not my hour for seeing patients — I mean people.'

'I'm sorry if I did wrong!' Joan cried. 'But

if you knew how much it means to me — '

'I can do nothing for you now,' said Lancaster. The voice was harsh again, but curiously flat, as if he were trying to restrain his emotions and hold himself in; as if he were afraid ... but afraid of what? Not of his anger.

Joan was standing in front of him, and even then the appearance of the man had something pathological about it to her mind. There was not the least jauntiness or self-consciousness about him. He looked older than in the morning; depressed, and certainly ill. His eyes were very bright, and his face unnaturally pale. He was pressing his thumb and finger against the rim of the chair as if for support. Joan remembered the stories of his drinking habits, but she saw at once that he had not been drinking. She had attended too many alcoholic patients at the hospital to not be sure of that.

'Dr. Lancaster, my dismissal means the loss of all my prospects. I came to ask if you won't inquire about my record and then give me another chance,' said Joan. 'And I'm sorry if I came at an inconvenient time; but now that I'm here, I must request the courtesy of a final answer. I shan't come to you again.'

'I cannot answer you,' said Lancaster, as if speaking in his sleep. 'In the interests of discipline it is impossible to answer you now.'

Joan turned away. The flat refusal stunned her. And there was something preposterous about Lancaster's manner that was perfectly incomprehensible to her. What was the matter with him? Why did the room turn round and round?

Suddenly she felt Lancaster's hand on her arm. He was supporting her, helping her into a chair, and through the fog she saw a look of concern on his face.

'Now sit, Miss Wentworth,' he said in a new tone of decision. 'Sit quietly, I tell you. Wait a minute, and, when you're feeling composed, let me see if I can't help you.'

He drew his chair toward hers again and leaned toward her. 'I have not been feeling well,' he explained. 'I was not myself when I discharged you this morning. When I refused to discuss the matter with you, it was because it's an invariable rule that the nurses are not supposed to come to my house. Outside the hospital I see nobody connected with the hospital. But I'll see what I can do. The matter will have to go before the board now, I suppose. Why did you come away without your breakfast? Why didn't your folks insist on your having something to eat?'

'I have no people,' answered Joan. 'My mother died nearly two years ago. We came here from Lucas County, and she was taken ill soon after our arrival. I hoped to get my diploma and have my profession.'

'You had no breakfast and I discharged you for fainting, and your diploma means everything to you,' said Lancaster slowly, clasping his hands as if in thought. Then, with a decisive, odd gesture, he leaned still nearer Joan and dropped his voice as he spoke, as if he were afraid that the man in the next room would hear him.

'Remember this as long as you live,' he said. 'In this life, people are not penalized for incapacity, they are punished for being unfortunate. Are you unlucky, Miss Wentworth?'

'I — why, yes, I suppose I must be,' she answered, looking at Lancaster in growing astonishment, mixed with a little fear.

'And you have sympathy for the unfortunate? You — you said something like that just now; about wishing to be of help to others. Are you loyal and staunch?'

'I hope I am,' said Joan uneasily.

'If one is loyal to others, one does not fear one's own misfortunes,' said Lancaster. 'They rise out of some fault or weakness if one follows the trail far enough back into one's self. I've learned that, heaven knows. Miss Wentworth,' he ended suddenly, 'would you consider a temporary position while your case is under investigation by the board?'

'But they meet in a day or two, and then —'

'Would you consider it,' repeated Lancaster, 'if you could be of greater service than you know? Suppose I said to you as I am saying now, that you seem to me the best suited, by loyalty and good will, of all the nurses I know, to help — would you accept?'

'Then, Dr. Lancaster,' cried Joan, triumphantly, 'if you have that opinion of me, you have no excuse for not getting the board to reinstate me!'

The man faltered as she looked at him. He was no longer terrible to her. He seemed to have put off some hateful armor that he had assumed and revealed weakness that none had suspected. Pity for him, a vast and heartfelt pity whose cause she was unable to divine, began to stir in Joan's heart.

'I pledge you my word to do all I can for you,' said Lancaster. 'But you must help me in turn. I need you for this purpose. I want you to go into the country for a month. It will rest you, too, and you are run down. Have you ever heard of the Lancaster Institute in Drexham County?'

'I think so,' answered Joan rather doubtfully.

'It's a hobby of mine. My father established it twenty-five years ago for the hill people, but the funds were squandered, and it's not in good shape. However, it does some good, and it's the only place of its kind within a score of miles. Dr. Jenkins is in charge, and I — I run down there every now and then to keep him up to the mark. There's a matron there. The cases comprise a little light surgical work occasionally, an alcoholic or two after pay days for the mining element, pneumonia in its season, and — yes, there's a mentally ill woman there, but she won't come under your care. It's in the hill country. How would you like to go?'

'I don't know what to say,' answered Joan.

'But you have no attachments in Avonmouth?' he asked, looking hard at her.

'Nobody. But, Dr. Lancaster, all my thoughts are bent on my reinstatement.'

'I'll do my very best for you if you'll help me out with this case,' he answered. 'And you'll get strong in a month and take up your work again with a light heart. You'll have a small remuneration, and your fare, of course. You'll go?'

'I'll go, then,' answered Joan.

'Then listen to me,' he said, again speaking with lowered voice and glancing back in apprehension toward the inner door. 'I shall not see you before you start, but I'll rely on you. You must leave on the nine o'clock train tomorrow morning. And you must speak to nobody about this undertaking.'

'I shall say nothing, Dr. Lancaster. And I have to thank you with all my heart — '

He frowned at her. The curious indecision in his manner, and the furtiveness of the man, which still disquieted her, was in extraordinary contrast to Lancaster's appearance in the theater that morning, and to everything she had associated with him. She was utterly bewildered.

As she rose, Lancaster came very close to her, and now his voice was little more than a whisper. 'I'll wire Mrs. Fraser, the matron,' he said, 'and I'll have the buggy meet you at the station, Miss Wentworth. And I wish — '

But the door opened, and the attendant slouched into the room. He stared insolently at Joan. 'Dr. Lancaster —' he began.

'I'll see you when I'm alone, Myers,' answered Lancaster.

'Dr. Lancaster, will you please give me a few moments of your time?' said the man urgently, and underneath the plea Joan seemed to see the insolence and contempt in his heart. Suddenly the idea came to her that his must be the man whom Lancaster had berated in the consulting room.

She went out, and as soon as she was in the passage she heard the attendant begin to address Lancaster in excited tones. Then the inner door opened. She fancied there were three men after all. Somebody was speaking in high tones, and then Lancaster's deep, booming voice rang out: 'You're a fool! You don't know when you're well off. I tell you, I wash my hands of you. This is final … '

Joan could not help but hear. She had gone into the waiting room to pick up her gloves, which she had nervously unfastened and thrown into a chair. And as she emerged into the passage, all the time hearing the sounds of the quarreling voices, Myers came hurrying past. He did not see her. He ran to the door, flung it open, and rushed down the steps into the street. As she went along the passage, Joan saw him staring right and left; then, as she came out, he saw her and went toward her. She knew that it was she whom he had been seeking.

'What was it Dr. Lancaster was saying to you, Miss Wentworth, before I came in?' he asked in his rasping voice.

Joan stared at him in astonishment. Now she realized that she had mistaken him; he was not a servant but apparently a member of the doctor's household.

'Will you let me pass, please?' asked Joan, as he blocked the way.

'I want to know what the doctor was saying to you,' repeated the man doggedly.

'Are you going to refuse me passage?' demanded Joan, flushing with anger.

He stepped aside with a sneer and a mock bow. 'Very well, if that's your attitude,' he answered. 'I shall find out.'

Joan turned swiftly upon him. 'I don't know who you are, but I shall complain of you to Dr. Lancaster,' she said.

Myers looked at her and sneered and chuckled. Then, without a word, he went back into the doctor's room. And still the voices kept up their quarreling dialogue.

Joan found herself in the street in the twilight; and now the unreality of the absurd interview struck home to her. She tried to puzzle it out. Before she reached the boarding house, she thought she had her clue.

That Lancaster, the terror of the nurses, should have been unable to promise immediate reinstatement, his evident good will, his indecision, and illness were explicable only in one way. The man Myers must be a relative, the third man perhaps a nephew.

Lancaster had been supporting a worthless pair in idleness and had turned on them in exasperation. That was the meaning of his look of illness, his preoccupation the shock of some domestic discovery.

At any rate, she was satisfied with some such solution. And she was certain that if she pleased him with her mysterious mission, her reinstatement would follow. She went home happy, and Mrs. Webb read the news in her face the moment she opened the door.

'I knew it, my dear,' she exclaimed with pleasure. 'I knew that you could twist that old devil round your finger if you tried hard enough.'

'Mrs. Webb, it was nothing of the kind,' said Joan. 'And Dr. Lancaster is one of the kindest of men. He's going to try to have his decision reversed; and, Mrs. Webb, he's sending me to a sanitarium on a case in the meantime.'

She checked herself, suddenly remembering Lancaster's caution. But Mrs. Webb took the woman to her wide bosom and kissed her.

'You little humbug,' she said.

'Mrs. Webb!' cried Joan, scandalized. 'If you knew — '

But when she was upstairs, she sat down suddenly and faced her conscience. What impression of herself had she given in the consulting room? She did not know. This scene, like that of the morning, had become blurred in her memory, and time had begun to flow very fast after the slowness of her twenty-two years. Certainly stranger things had happened to her that day than at any time since her mother's death.

She leaned out of the window. It was growing hot again, but the awnings down the street were flapping in a strengthening breeze, and the park looked inviting in the late evening. She suddenly remembered that the institute was not many miles from her old home. It would be almost going home — and on the morrow. Joy leaped into her heart.

Then she saw something that for an instant chilled the blood in her veins. Across the street, leaning against the park railings and looking up at the house, was the short square-built figure of a man wearing a hard hat. She could not distinguish the face, but she thought it was Myers. And she remembered his threat.

What did it mean? Bewildered, she turned into her room again. She half-regretted now that she was to go to Lancaster.

But in the morning she dismissed the incident from her mind as a fantasy.

3

Joan Makes a Promise

At half past seven in the evening, Joan descended from the train at Lancaster station after an all-day ride. At first she had passed through the network of coastal towns and villages, then the tilled fields just north of the cotton belt, rich with green corn; then the peach orchards, and finally the woodland, broken by patches of cultivated country.

It was like going home. Joan could not see her village, which was on a branch line, but at Medlington she was only four miles away. There were the same misty mountains breaking the horizon line; the same small, straggling towns; the same fragrance of the deep forests, bringing back to her those remembrances which a chance odor suddenly unlooses, as at the touch of some magician's staff. The two years that she had spent at Avonmouth seemed to slip out of her recollection.

As the afternoon flew by, the distant mountains changed into a semicircle of irregular heights. Now the train was climbing into the foothills. It was a lonely land. This was further in the back country than Joan had ever been. The villages were becoming mere clusters of cabins. There had been two changes of trains, and each time the coach became shabbier and more disreputable and more impregnated with tobacco smoke.

The character of Joan's fellow travelers changed as well. They were more uncouth, with chin beards and rough store suits; they sat perspiring and collarless, the soft hats pulled over their foreheads. But she looked at them with the loving appreciation of her own people that was in her heart, and they, in the presence of the pretty woman who was traveling alone, displayed the innate courtesy of the southerner.

The sun descended; it was gilding the whole land with level rays of gold and dancing on the horizon like a red ball when the train pulled into Lancaster, the last station before Millville, the terminus. Joan got down and looked about her.

The station was a tiny place and seemed deserted. The booking office was closed. In the waiting room, appearing almost to fill it, was a stout black woman with a dozen parcels; from the wicker sides of one, two hens' heads with blinking eyes protruded. Outside, a ramshackle buggy with a lean chestnut horse attached was drawn up to the edge of the muddy road.

A well-dressed young mountain boy in a hard felt hat was standing beside it. As Joan came out of the station he turned toward her, took off his hat, and bowed. 'Miss Wentworth?' he inquired in a well-bred tone.

'Yes. You're from the institute?'

'Yes, Miss Wentworth. Mrs. Fraser will be expecting you.' He looked beyond her, and Joan, turning, perceived to her discomfiture the man Myers in his hard hat. He must have traveled up in the train with her.

Myers came forward, taking off his hat grudgingly. 'Miss Wentworth, I'm sorry if I annoyed you last night,' he said. 'I ought to have explained to you that I'm the secretary of the institution. I guess my manners aren't very good, but I meant no harm.'

Joan, who had witnessed his presence with consternation, now felt a sudden re-action from her fears. Of course, Myers' explanation made the situation intelligible. She bowed, and he turned to the boy.

'You can take Miss Wentworth up,' he said. 'I'll find a buggy somewhere.'

As there was only room for two in the buggy, Joan did not demur to the prop-osition. She stepped in, the young man holding out his hand to guard her dress from the wheel. Joan glanced at the man with momentary interest. He had the man-ners of a gentleman. There was no hint of either servility or presumption, and yet there was a sort of independence about the man which fitted him admirably. He flicked the horse, and the buggy began to crawl out of the station yard along the single street of a tiny village, straggling uphill.

It was a charming village, though there were clusters of shanties a little back among the pines. There was a store or two, their fronts plastered with tobacco and baking powder advertisements, and in front of one stood a gaunt, yellow-faced hill man chewing and gazing after the buggy with an unanimated face.

'This is Lancaster?' asked Joan.

'Yes, Miss Wentworth.'

'The people here look depressed.'

'There's a good deal of sickness, Miss Wentworth. Hookworm, and what they used to call malaria. But there isn't any malaria here; it's bad diet — salt pork and soda biscuits. And there's pellagra; it's been here for generations, but it wasn't till last year that the medical commission discovered it.'

The coachman's knowledge might have been ludicrous in most men of his class, but there was nothing ridiculous in the grave, refined face of the young mountaineer. He must have picked up some knowledge at the institute, thought Joan.

'But it's healthy up in the hills, Miss Wentworth,' he added. 'This village is Millville. They used to grow cotton in the valley over yonder, but the frost killed the crops three years ago, and the mill fell into ruin. Quite a little water power in the stream.'

The buggy ascended a steeper grade,

the horse breaking into a short gallop near every summit, and then resuming its leisurely crawl.

'That's the institute, Miss Wentworth,' the coachman continued, pointing toward a straggling building on a little plateau. It had the appearance of a large but rather dilapidated farmhouse. 'It's three miles by the road,' he added, 'but less than a mile over the hills.'

The horse had stopped to gain breath again. Looking back, Joan saw a white line that crept upward over the rocky slopes almost direct from the station to the building. Halfway up was a little speck of black that seemed to move. Joan knew it was Myers's hard hat, his body being hidden from view among the bushes. She shuddered slightly; the man was very repugnant to her.

The horse went on again, the road winding uphill through pastures gay with buttercups and white with little branched asters.

The buggy came to a standstill before the long wooden building, which was of unshingled boards and much the worse for weather. It had not been painted for years, and two windows in one wing were broken. A patch of weedy, unmown lawn extended between what had once been hedges but were now mere tangles of undergrowth.

Nearby was a large enclosure in which were a few chickens pecking for grains of corn; and a cow at pasture turned her head and gazed at them placidly.

The door opened and a pleasant-looking woman came forward. 'How do you do, Miss Wentworth?' she said. 'I'm the matron, Mrs. Fraser. Dr. Lancaster telegraphed about your coming. I'll show you your room, and your supper will be ready in a few minutes.'

Joan descended. The driver, who had leaped to the ground, held his hand over the wheel, but did not offer it to her. Then he re-entered the buggy, and, rather to Joan's surprise, drove off along the road by which they had ascended.

The woman, after a moment's hesitation, preceded Mrs. Fraser into the building. She saw a long corridor with a number of doors on either side and the stairs in front of her.

'You would like to see the building, Miss

Wentworth?' asked the matron. 'Or perhaps you're tired and would prefer to go to your room.'

'No, I should like to see it. Have you many patients?'

'Only Mrs. Dana. She's always here, you know. There was a boy with a broken arm, but he left this morning. In winter, though, we're often crowded. It isn't much of a place, Miss Wentworth, but we do a little good. This is the doctor's apartment. He sleeps here; next door is the clinic, and next to that the operating room. Here we keep the supplies. This is my room. Mr. Myers, the secretary, has his room opposite the doctor's. This is the dining room, and here is the kitchen. Now I'll show you your room upstairs, Miss Wentworth.'

The corridor above was a replica of the one below. At the head of the stairs a little passage branched off toward a large window in the wall, with a door to one side of it.

'Mrs. Dana occupies this room,' said the matron. 'Perhaps the doctor mentioned her?'

'Dr. Lancaster said something — '

'She's out of her mind, poor woman,

but she's perfectly quiet. You see, Miss Wentworth, she's like an infant mentally. She won't trouble you. Excuse me a moment.'

She drew a key from the bunch that hung at her waist and unlocked the door softly and with a certain furtiveness, Joan thought. Looking in, she saw a strikingly handsome woman of about seven and thirty years seated in a chair beside a window, with a shawl over her knees. She was in a dressing gown and her hair hung over her shoulders in two braids. She did not look up or stir as the matron entered, and Mrs. Fraser, after closing the door behind her, presently came out and locked it again.

'I'll show you your room now, Miss Wentworth,' she said. 'You'll be alone on this floor except for Mrs. Dana, but you're not afraid of her?'

'Not in the least. Is she incurable?'

'Yes, quite, poor thing. She's sat in that chair all day for nearly three years.'

'And she never goes out?'

'Out? No, we don't let her out. It might excite her. But I'm not supposed to speak about the cases. It's very sad, though. She comes of a good family, but they neglected her when she was in trouble, and she's as good as dead to everyone now. She never speaks, but I don't know whether she could. I've never heard her since I came here three years ago. This is the ward. And this is your room.'

The open doors along the corridor had revealed clean little rooms with iron bedsteads and plain furniture; the room at the end of the passage, however, was well furnished, with a heavy new carpet and old mahogany furniture. Outside the window, through the twilight, appeared the distant mountains.

Joan, turning, was surprised to see Mrs. Fraser watching her intently. As their eyes met, the matron lowered her own in some confusion. There was a furtiveness about her glance that momentarily revived Joan's uneasiness. It was a strange journey, and Dr. Lancaster's behavior had been also strange. Then there was the man Myers. Joan felt a sudden sinking of the heart; she was almost regretful that she had come.

A maid brought up her suitcase. 'This is Lucy,' said the matron. 'She'll do anything you tell her. She sleeps overhead in the attic. And my room is underneath,' she added, 'so if you should want anything at any time, just tap on the radiator and I'll come up at once. And supper will be ready as soon as you are.'

In the hall, Joan found Mrs. Fraser ten minutes later, talking to the secretary. 'Miss Wentworth, this is Mr. Myers,' she began.

'We've met already,' said Myers, scrutinizing her closely. He seemed now to wear the same furtive air as Mrs. Fraser; it seemed part of the atmosphere of the institution. Joan had perceived it in the coachman, too.

'Miss Wentworth is to have charge of the nursing under Dr. Jenkins,' said Mrs. Fraser.

'I hope I shan't conflict with — ' began Joan doubtfully.

'Not at all, not at all,' said Myers, speaking with false heartiness. 'I hope we shall all get along well together.'

Joan refused to face the problem of Myers's undoubted hostility. One must live for the moment; that she had discovered in her first days at the Southern. She went into the dining room and found to her relief that the table was only laid for one.

'Mr. Myers has had supper?' she asked.

'You are to have your meals alone, Miss Wentworth,' answered the matron.

'But I should not wish — '

'It is the doctor's orders,' said Mrs. Fraser in a tone of finality.

Coming in with the dessert, Mrs. Fraser found Joan nodding at the table. She had begun to feel an intense fatigue after the all-day journey. She began to realize, too, that her work at the hospital had been harder than she had thought. 'I believe I shall go straight to bed,' she said.

'The best thing you can do, Miss Wentworth. Everybody feels sleepy when they first arrive here. It's the hill air. You must rest well; and please remember, it's you who give the orders.'

She preceded Joan up the stairs, carrying an oil lamp. She set it down in Joan's room, and then she seemed to hesitate. 'Miss Wentworth,' she said, 'the doctor wants us to do everything we can to make you comfortable. There isn't likely to be any work unless some patient comes in. You were not to attend Mrs. Dana, I think?'

'I was told not.'

'That's so, Miss Wentworth.' The matron's air was a very decided one, and again she conveyed the impression of something hidden which was, further, meant to remain hidden. 'The doctor wired me that. I don't suppose he said anything about Mrs. Dana to you? Or Mr. Myers?' Her stealthy watchfulness now seemed of ominous portent, and the matron made no attempt to suppress the eagerness with which she awaited Joan's answer.

'No, Dr. Lancaster said nothing,' Joan said. Then, seeing that the matron was still regarding her doubtfully, she added: 'But is not Dr. Jenkins resident here? I haven't seen him yet.'

The matron stared at her in astonishment. 'Why, Miss Wentworth, that was Dr. Jenkins who drove you up from the station.'

'That was Dr. Jenkins?'

'I thought Dr. Lancaster would have told you about him. He's a graduate of Johns Hopkins. Old Dr. Lancaster wanted to build up an institution here where we hill people could work among our own. But the plan fell through. You see, the hospital in Avonmouth got hold of most of the money, and then — there were other difficulties. I don't know about them — I've only been here three years, and Dr. Jenkins wasn't graduated then, and we never pay attention to the gossip of the villagers.' She checked herself hastily, as if she was afraid of compromising herself. 'Dr. Jenkins has given up his life to the work here,' she continued. 'He lives at Millville, but we hope that Dr. Lancaster will build up the place again, if only he … ' There was almost a look of agony on her face, and again she turned her eyes upon Joan's face as if to search out her thoughts. Then, with an abrupt 'Good night,' she turned away.

Joan called to her as she was leaving the room. 'Mrs. Fraser,' she said, 'I understood that there was a patient here besides Mrs. Dana.'

The matron turned slowly around. 'There was the boy who left this morning,' she said inquiringly.

'But I understood from Dr. Lancaster — at least, he didn't tell me in so many words, but he gave me to understand that there was a special case here requiring care and sympathy.'

The matron stared at her. 'No, there's nobody,' she said. 'Nobody except — ' Suddenly she uttered a convulsive sound and, putting her hands over her face, ran from the room. Joan heard her stumbling down the corridor outside as if she had gone blind.

She stood irresolute in her room. Her sleepiness was gone; she was afraid, and she seemed to have got out of her depth. It had begun with John Lancaster's strange behavior in his office the evening before. She had not been able then to reconcile him in any way with the Lancaster whom she had seen, smug and self-satisfied and vain, in the operating room, the bully who kept the nurses in agitation and fear, though he was the traditional John Lancaster of whom she had heard. Then there was the man Myers, equally strange; and the matron. Some mystery was at the heart of it all; and Joan was the more afraid because the reason for her fear was unknown to her.

Her sleepiness was gone. She stood beside the window, looking out into the darkness. A whippoorwill was calling monotonously among the pines, and here and there among the hills a solitary light was twinkling. The air was cool and balsam-scented. It was like the dearly remembered days at home. But in the heart of that peace was apprehension.

Looking back now, Joan thought that she had undertaken a rash and extraordinary adventure in coming so far from Avonmouth alone and at the proposal of a man whose reputation was an evil one. She would go home on the morrow. Something was wrong; and in spite of his apparent kindness, an inner prompting warned her to beware of Lancaster. He was at the heart of all this and had enmeshed her in some scheme for his own purposes.

She locked her door and went to bed, to sleep restlessly. When she awakened, it was morning. The sun was streaming brightly into the room. Through the window Joan saw a scene of exquisite beauty in the rolling hills, the winding road, the forest glades. Underneath, the chickens were scrambling for corn which the matron was flinging to them. A thousand birds were calling, the universal robin and the bluebird of her beloved home. The dew lay heavy on the leaves and grass. Joan felt a sudden ecstasy. This was her own country, and she had come back to it. Her fears were dissipated with the night shadows.

She would remain. She decided this while she was dressing, and yet doubt remained in her heart; and with it came the remembrance of something that had disturbed her during the night. Filtering into her consciousness came the recollection of an automobile rolling up to the door, and of men's voices conversing in low tones under her window. Then the machine had rolled away. It must have been about two in the morning. Perhaps a patient had been brought to the institute, thought Joan, as she went downstairs.

Mrs. Fraser's door was closed and the only person astir seemed to be the maid Lucy, who nodded and smiled as she looked up from her sweeping. Joan began to pace the long veranda in front of the building, looking out across the hills and thinking over her situation.

Perhaps it was only morbidness, or

mental fatigue, that had made her read things in the faces of Myers and Mrs. Fraser which did not exist there. Perhaps the day would disclose her position more definitely.

She was walking past the open door of the building when she saw a man leaving the doctor's room. It was Myers, the secretary. He saw Joan and came briskly out upon the veranda. 'Good morning, Miss Wentworth,' he said in his rasping tones. 'Pleasant weather, isn't it? Much hotter here than in Avonmouth.'

'How do you do, Mr. Myers?' said Joan, trying to overcome her instinctive disgust of the man. 'You have a new patient here, haven't you?'

He looked at her with a sort of quizzical shrewdness. 'What makes you think that, Miss Wentworth?' he inquired.

'I thought I heard an auto drive up to the institute last night.'

His expression did not change. 'The doctor came back last night unexpectedly.'

'But I thought Dr. Jenkins lived at Millville?'

'Not Jenkins, Miss Wentworth. Dr. Lancaster.'

'Why,' stammered Joan, 'I must have misunderstood, then. I thought you were working in cooperation with Dr. Jenkins. I hope Dr. Lancaster is not ill. He was looking unwell when I saw him the day before yesterday.'

'That's just what you might have told me when I asked you about him,' said Myers triumphantly. 'Well, Miss Wentworth, if you're going to ask me questions, I suppose I can ask you questions?'

'If I can answer them.'

'Precisely. Now let's be frank. What do you know about all this?'

'I beg your pardon?' Joan inquired, declining his invitation to seat herself beside him.

'Come, now, you know what I mean as well as I do. How did Dr. Lancaster come to engage you?'

'If you really have a right to know, Mr. Myers,' said Joan, 'you had better ask Dr. Lancaster himself.'

'Oh, all right,' said Myers huffily. 'But the time will come when you'll wish you'd been frank with me. If we put all our cards on the table, we can have a good look into the situation.'

'Really, Mr. Myers, I had no idea that I had come to a gambling house,' said Joan, more nettled by the familiarity of his tone than by the words. 'I have no cards at all, as you term it. I am simply an employee of Dr. Lancaster, and if that is not satisfactory to you, I must refer you to him.'

Myers grew red. His short, stocky figure with wide shoulders looked abominably mean as he planted himself upon the porch and surveyed Joan with a furtive, sneering expression. He was not in any sense a gentleman, just a low class of bully, as Joan could plainly see from his gestures, even if his next words had not made this plain.

'So that's your attitude, is it?' he said, jerking out the words between his teeth. 'All right, Miss Wentworth, you and I will play our hands separately. Don't come to me afterward, though, and say I didn't warn you. And if you don't like my ways and speech, and think I'm too ordinary for your taste — here comes the doctor! Go and make a complaint about me!'

Joan, turning from the man in disgust, saw Dr. Lancaster standing at the door.

She went toward him, and then she looked at him in consternation. For Lancaster was undeniably ill. His face was a dead white, and he was leaning on a stick, as if to support himself.

'Dr. Lancaster — ' she began.

He straightened himself with an effort, held out his hand, and took her own. 'I'm very glad you came, Miss Wentworth,' he said. 'I hope you like the institute?'

Myers, who had come up and planted himself between them, flung out his challenge. 'She likes the institute all right, Doctor,' he said with a short laugh, 'but I reckon she doesn't like me. Bad taste, I call it. What do you say, Doctor?'

There was an indescribable insolence in the man's tone. Joan looked for one of Lancaster's explosions of flaming wrath, but to her amazement none came. He seemed to be struggling to control himself. He flushed and looked from one to the other.

'Well, well, Myers,' he said, hesitating, 'I think things will turn out all right. Miss Wentworth and you won't conflict in any way. You mustn't quarrel, you know. I want all my employees to like each other,' he ended weakly.

He gave Joan an impression of pitiful impotence, as if he were somehow in the secretary's power and had surrendered his will to him — Lancaster, the tyrant of the Southern Hospital, the smug bully of the operating theater! Joan saw a flash of triumph in Myers's eyes, and, with another laugh, the man left them and went into the building.

'I think breakfast is ready, Miss Wentworth,' said Lancaster after a moment, offering her his arm. But Joan gave him hers instead, and they went together into the dining room.

She was glad to see that Myers was not to eat with them. Hungry as she was, she could not have taken breakfast in the man's presence; and even now she could hardly manage to eat with Lancaster, so evidently ill, seated opposite her, swallowing gulps of hot coffee and making a pretense of eating thin strips of toast. His whole demeanor was that of a very ill man. And the transformation terrified her. All her preconceived ideas of him had vanished. She could make nothing of him. She felt a deep sense of relief when the meal ended.

Then Lancaster looked at her with the same furtive expression that she read in the face of everybody there. 'I thought I would run up and see how the institute was getting along, Miss Wentworth,' he said.

They had risen from the table. Joan turned and faced him. 'Dr. Lancaster, you spend a good deal of your time here. There was nothing unexpected about your visit last night. You knew that you would come here when you employed me.'

She must have spoken more angrily than she knew, for the web of deception was smothering her, and she felt that her position was becoming unendurable. For an instant a glimmer of amusement passed over the doctor's face.

'Why, Miss Wentworth, you're a regular spitfire,' he said.

'It is true, then?'

'Well — yes, it's true. My work at Avonmouth is not too exacting for me to come here frequently.'

'You knew you were coming, and you didn't tell me. And you hinted at a patient requiring care. There is no patient, unless it is yourself. Dr. Lancaster, you engaged me for certain work here, and I am ready to fulfill it. It's not necessary for you to explain anything to me. But please give me the work you hired me to do, and don't try to deceive me.'

Lancaster, who had been regarding her intently as she spoke, glanced hurriedly into the hall before replying. A look of fear had come into his eyes. Joan knew that it was Myers whom he feared. There was something dreadful in seeing this man cringe before the bully — this man who had, in turn, made others cringe before him.

'Miss Wentworth,' said Lancaster in a low tone, 'believe me, I have no intention of deceiving you. On the contrary, it is my wish to confide in you. Will you come out on the porch and permit me to smoke?'

She bowed, and they went out together. They took their seats upon two chairs at the end of the veranda, Joan purposely seating herself between her companion and the door. She knew why he kept glancing toward it.

'Miss Wentworth,' Lancaster began, 'we spoke of loyalty the other night. If you saw a human being in trouble of his own making, would it be your impulse to help him, or to leave him to fight his battle alone?'

'I should help him if I could,' said Joan.

'Then help me,' said Lancaster. 'It was myself of whom I spoke. Will you help me with loyalty and sympathy, and refuse to be discouraged?'

Joan softened toward him; he was obviously sincere and distressed. 'Gladly, Dr. Lancaster,' she answered.

'I thought that I could trust you when I saw your face, and I was sure of it when you talked of your vocation. And I cannot trust anyone else. I have had no opportunity — ' He broke off irresolutely and went on. 'I have had no opportunity of taking up that matter with the board yet,' he continued.

Joan knew that he was not speaking frankly now, but his next words were in the same tone of sincerity.

'Miss Wentworth, that matter and this are all bound up together. You must help me before I can help you, as I said to you when you came into the consulting room. I can't explain any more now. I want help in the biggest fight of my life, and if I fail, I want a witness that I have fought. I saw you and thought you would give me your help. For God's sake, don't refuse me!'

In spite of his sincerity, the idea flashed through Joan's mind that his troubles might be the fancies of a sick man.

'If I discharge you before the month is over, don't go. Refuse to go. Nobody can make you go. I am the head of the institute. Ignore me. Stay!'

'I'll stay,' said Joan; and then, looking at his white face and trembling hands, she thought she knew what was the matter with him. 'Listen, Dr. Lancaster,' she said, laying her fingers on his arm. But then she saw that he was not looking at her. He was looking past her to Myers, who was coming across the pasture toward the entrance. His expression was transformed.

'Miss Wentworth,' he said with a sudden change of tone, 'what was I saying to you? I'm not myself at all today. I've been greatly overworked, and am talking nonsense. Don't remember it. I meant nothing at all. Of course you must remain for the entirety your month, in case any patients come, and then we'll see what we can do about the position.'

As Myers came up to them, the same hopeless, cringing expression came into his eyes. The secretary ignored Joan completely.

'Well, Doctor,' he said, 'I have the quarterly statement ready for you. Won't you come and look it over? I must have your signature, and you know how hard it is to fasten you down.'

'Yes, I'll come, certainly, Myers,' said Lancaster, rising.

4

Joan and Myers Clash

The two men went into the house together. Joan heard the door close behind them. She was left to ponder over that interview.

She was conscious of two conflicting impulses: to leave, or to remain for Lancaster's sake. There was something about the man's pitiable condition that aroused all her sympathies. But there was something about the whole place that was repulsive in the extreme. She must get allies in this blind fight against the secretary if she remained. But who? Mrs. Fraser? That was impossible as yet.

At that moment she saw Dr. Jenkins driving up the path and went to meet him. He sprang to the ground and raised his hat. 'Good morning. Miss Wentworth. How is the doctor today?' he asked.

'Dr. Lancaster looks very ill. And, Dr. Jenkins, I want to ask you — '

'Pardon me, Miss Wentworth, but can I see him?'

'He's with Mr. Myers.'

Jenkins's face assumed an aspect of profound discouragement. 'Then I'll come back this afternoon,' he said, preparing to enter the buggy again.

But he found Joan intercepting his passage. She had noted the look on his face, and she felt that he understood much which could be explained. 'Dr. Jenkins,' she said quietly, 'Dr. Lancaster is unwell, and I'm his nurse. Will you tell me what the matter is with him?'

'Why, Miss Wentworth — ' stammered the doctor.

'There's no reason why you shouldn't see him because he happens to be with Mr. Myers.'

'Well, Miss Wentworth, you see, Mr. Myers is his secretary, and there's always a lot of business to be done.'

'Dr. Jenkins, Dr. Lancaster is in no condition to attend to business. What's wrong with him?'

The doctor looked right and left, as if trying to find some refuge. But Joan was standing in front of him, and he could not enter the buggy without pushing her away.

'Miss Wentworth, please don't ask me about the doctor,' he said. 'I do my best for him. It isn't in my power to do more than I already am.'

'It's in your power to help him to be master of himself. How can the most famous surgeon in the south come here and be at the mercy of a man like Myers?'

'Why, Miss Wentworth, you've got that wrong,' protested Jenkins. 'Mr. Myers is only the secretary. He does all he can for the doctor. We've got to keep the institute together, and we're each doing our best. You see, the trust fund wasn't made over to the doctor. He was only in charge of it, and when the money went missing it worried him. And — and — ' He stopped, as if he had caught himself babbling about something that should not have been mentioned. Then, as Joan stood aside, he leaped into the vehicle. 'Good morning,' he muttered, raising his hat, and drove away furiously.

She went back to the veranda. She was resolved to reach the bottom of the mystery for Lancaster's sake; to prove her loyalty, although he had withdrawn his demand on her.

As she reached the front door, she was startled to hear her name spoken in the matron's room. The speaker was Myers.

'But she knows nothing at all,' Mrs. Fraser was saying.

'She knows a good deal too much,' Myers answered.

'What do you suppose the doctor brought her here for if not to try to publish his shame to the world? Aye, his shame,' repeated the matron bitterly. 'It's hard work for three people to try to hold up one man without a fourth coming in.'

'Well, is that his game?' demanded the secretary. 'Is it or isn't it?'

'We want a nurse. You know we've often tried to get one, Mr. Myers, but they won't stay here. It's hard work taking care of the patients sometimes when there's a rush.'

'Rush!' repeated Myers scornfully. 'Who'd rush to this old place with the doctor's reputation?'

'They do come, and the people trust him,' said Mrs. Fraser, half-crying.

'Yes,' scoffed the other. 'And the doctor still has his grandiose ideas about building up the institution — him that wrecked it.'

'Well, that woman knows nothing, anyway.'

'I tell you she means to help the doctor in his crazy plan of notoriety. She means to undo all our work in his own interests,' cried Myers vehemently.

Joan walked away. She had overheard unwillingly, and enough to convince her that there was a mystery, with Myers at the bottom of it. She had rightly sensed an energy in him, as he in her. Now her mind was resolute to remain and fight for Lancaster.

But she had not passed the entrance when the matron's door swung open violently and Myers came out. He stood confronting Joan with his insulting leer.

'Miss Wentworth,' he began, 'when you and I had our talk this morning, you hadn't seen the doctor. You didn't know how things were situated, and I don't blame you. Now you've seen that the doctor needs a guardian. Well, I'm his guardian.'

'I don't think Dr. Lancaster needs a

guardian, Mr. Myers,' answered Joan, facing him steadily.

'See here now, Miss Wentworth,' said Myers, swallowing hard. 'You don't get the drift of things, just as I thought. You think I'm trying to stand in the way of your work, when I'm only trying to reach a sort of working agreement to keep things in running order. That's my aim. Am I right?'

'I don't know if you're right. I think you're extremely uncivil. Take off your hat!' flashed Joan.

Myers removed the hard hat from his head and stared at her in astonishment. He could not understand her sudden initiation of hostilities.

'Well, I reckon that's my nature, and I'm sorry,' he said. He was trying to be conciliatory now. 'I'm sorry if I got on your nerves, Miss Wentworth,' he persisted, 'but I was not brought up to be a ladies' man. However, I know my job, and I reckon you know yours. If you think I'm trying to stand between the doctor and you, come and see him right now.'

'I have no complaint to make, and I have made none,' said Joan.

'Come and see him,' persisted Myers. 'You're the nurse, and I guess it's up to you.'

She looked at him, dismayed by his expression. 'Is Dr. Lancaster worse?' she asked.

'Well, nothing that I didn't expect, but he might be better,' said Myers, sneering.

He walked toward the door of Lancaster's room and opened it. Through the aperture Joan saw Lancaster stretched out in a large chair, his head bent forward on his breast, his limbs immobile. She hurried into the room.

But Myers preceded her to Lancaster's side. He raised the limp arm and turned up the sleeve. Joan saw that the skin was densely scarred with little punctures. Lancaster was breathing heavily. Beside him upon a little table was a syringe, and near that a little bottle containing a few drops of a pale fluid. Joan drew in her breath quickly. It was what she had feared.

'Morphine,' said Myers. 'He always does this when he comes home. Now you understand what I was trying to get at this morning, Miss Wentworth. I'm responsible for him. It's my job to keep him straight, if I can. When I can't, I try. Now you see, perhaps, why he's lost his willpower, and why I have to keep after him like a dog following its master. And I guess you won't think I'm trying to set him against you.' The bully in the man was coming to the surface again. He thrust out his head toward Joan. 'Because if you do, I may as well say, Miss Wentworth, that I'm the boss here. Understand that?' he continued with a blustering air. 'The doctor hires all sorts of people when he's like this, and it doesn't mean anything. He can't pay out any salaries unless my signature is on the vouchers. We want a nurse, and if you'd like to stay on you can. But if you stay, you help me so far as the doctor's concerned, and you do what I tell you. Is that clear?'

Joan looked at him indifferently. 'Help me put Dr. Lancaster on the bed,' she said, 'and then run and get me a hot water bottle.'

He scowled furiously, but obeyed her. While Joan sat at Lancaster's side, watching him, her mind ran over the questions that were puzzling her. She sat for hours beside the sick man, conscious sometimes that Myers had come in and spoken to her, but she never answered him. As the pulse strengthened, she let her mind work upon the problem again.

Lancaster had taken an immense overdose, one inconceivable in the ordinary morphine habitué. And he must have taken it during the brief period when Myers was with him; he must have taken it as soon as he got back into his room. Why had Myers permitted it?

At last Lancaster opened his eyes. His gaze fell upon Joan's face, at first without recognition, then with wonder. 'Water!' he gasped after a few ineffectual attempts to speak.

Joan drew a glassful and gave it to him, and then another. Lancaster gulped down the liquid greedily. Presently he sat up, stood on his feet, and groped his way to the chair.

'I'm sorry,' he said, looking at Joan with a whimsical expression. 'I should have told you.'

'Dr. Lancaster, I am ashamed of you,' said Joan.

'God knows I'm ashamed of myself,' he burst out fretfully. 'Miss Wentworth, in the third drawer of that desk, beneath a pile of letters, you'll find a bottle — '

'No,' said Joan decisively.

She knew by the wholly unnecessary secrecy in the concealment, characteristic of the drug habitué, that Lancaster had gone a long way down the declivity.

'Miss Wentworth, you misunderstand me. It's an antidote for alkaloid poisoning. I was experimenting with a new drug.'

Joan found herself sobbing, and she was astonished. It was the wreck of the man's moral nature that was unbearable. She saw the latent fineness in him, and it was as if the needless lie was the voice of the morphine devil that spoke through his lips.

Lancaster looked distressed. 'Miss Wentworth, you'd better leave me and go back to Avonmouth on the next train,' he said. 'I ought never to have brought you here. It was pure selfishness on my part. Please don't cry. Go away now, and we'll talk it over before you start for the station.'

'If I go away,' wept Joan, 'you'll take another hypodermic.'

'I pledge you my word of honor no,' said Lancaster, with almost ingenuous candor. 'I'm really not accustomed to such a thing; that's why it knocked me out. I've been suffering from insomnia, and I tried a new alkaloid — not morphine, you know, but a derivative for the benefit of my patients.'

'Your word of honor!' said Joan.

He leaned back in his chair and looked at her with amusement. 'Miss Wentworth,' he said, 'you're a nurse. Surely you're aware that I'm not to be trusted; that my word of honor is worthless? That I am essentially devoid of honesty and decency? Don't you know that this accursed thing — ' He pointed toward the bottle. ' — robs men of their honor and self-respect, and lowers them beneath the beasts?'

'That does not refer to you,' answered Joan. 'You asked me to help you in the biggest fight of your life. Well, I'm going to help you in that fight!'

'It's too late,' said Lancaster.

'Never!' replied Joan valiantly.

'You don't understand, Miss Wentworth. That's the mistake all people make in trying to cure us. Don't you know that a man or woman never becomes a victim to a drug except from sleeplessness, or physical pain, or under stress of mortal anguish? If you could cure me, the old trouble would still be there. I should fall a victim again. Life is worthless to me, Miss Wentworth,' he ended, quite simply.

'For happiness, perhaps; I don't know. But not for duty. Your life is to be used, Dr. Lancaster, for the sake of the people, and I'm going to help you use it. Your wonderful skill — '

He groaned at the words. Joan saw that, though he was suffering physically, there was some mental trouble which her words had evoked. 'Dr. Lancaster,' she said, 'the first thing you have to do is use your will. And I'm going to give you your first test, a little one only. It will last thirty seconds. Can you put forth your will for just that length of time?'

He fixed his eyes anxiously on hers and nodded. Yet she saw them waver toward the bottle.

'I'm going to cross the room,' she said. 'Don't stir a finger till I return.'

She had heard Myers in the hall, and,

going to the door, she turned the key. She heard Myers halt near her door. But she had no time to think of him. She went back to Lancaster, whose hands were strained hard against the arms of the chair.

'Well done!' she said.

'Miss Wentworth, I must have that hypodermic now.'

'I want you to wait. Wait half an hour, Dr. Lancaster.'

'I can't!' he cried, starting up. 'I tell you I must have it. After an overdose one must have a smaller one. It will set me up nicely. Just half the quantity, Miss Wentworth.'

'In half an hour,' said Joan.

He sprang to his feet, shaking and furious. 'Give me that bottle at once!' he cried.

'In half an hour.'

Lancaster sat down. 'Confound you, why ever did you come here?' he asked. 'Suppose I discharge you?'

'I won't go, Dr. Lancaster. We've covered that point in our conversation already.' Then, seeing his distress, she went on rapidly: 'Listen to me, Dr. Lancaster. You brought me here upon an impulse because you had no one whom you could trust. You wanted to fight, and you wanted me to fight with you. Well, I'm going to do it, and we're going to win.' She took out her watch and laid it on the table. 'In twenty-five minutes you shall have half a dose. Then we shall have won the first skirmish. Oh, Dr. Lancaster, fight like a man and help us win!'

She spoke with so much earnestness that she kindled his enthusiasm. 'Yes, we'll make the fight!' he cried, with blazing eyes. 'If only I had had you long ago.' He was in the full reaction from his despondency. He struck his fist emphatically upon the arm of the chair. 'I'll be a man again!' he cried. 'If you knew everything, Miss Wentworth, you might understand how a man can be caught in a snare of his own making. But I'll win, with your aid, and I'll be my own master again.'

'You are your own master now, Dr. Lancaster. Always think that and remember it.'

'My own master? When that hound follows me — '

'Mr. Myers is your servant.'

Lancaster laughed harshly. 'By Heaven!' he cried. 'I'll tell him so. Miss Wentworth, give me that dose now so that I can feel like a man again and have the strength to send him about his business.'

'It will give you strength,' she answered, 'but it will not make you yourself, your better self. You will no longer want to send him about his business.'

Lancaster stared at her. 'How do you know that?' he asked. 'It's true. But I can't wait any longer. I've waited fifteen minutes. Half an hour next time. Miss Wentworth, the third drawer — '

As her eyes went toward the desk, he snatched up the bottle and hypodermic from the table. Joan caught at his wrist, but Lancaster had already plunged the syringe into the fluid, and he was upon his feet. He tried to free his hand — he fought furiously — but Joan succeeded in knocking the bottle from his grasp. It fell upon the table. Lancaster righted it and suddenly darted toward the desk. Joan caught him. He flung her across the room. He had got the drawer open when she grappled with him again.

He struck at her with his right hand, beating her about the wrists, but she would not let go. She would never let go, not though he struck her in the face. He tossed her this way and that, but she never unclasped her hold. At last he dropped into his chair, exhausted, and covered his face with his hands.

'Twelve minutes more,' said Joan triumphantly, looking at her watch. Then she realized that all through the struggle there had been a hammering at the door. She got up. 'Who is it?' she called.

'Miss Wentworth, unlock the door, please,' came the frightened voice of Mrs. Fraser.

'In a few minutes,' said Joan.

'Miss Wentworth, what are you doing to Dr. Lancaster?'

'I'm taking care of him.'

'Mr. Myers says you'll kill him. He's got to have his morphine; you can't stop a man abruptly like that. Mr. Myers understands him — '

'Mr. Myers can come in in fifteen minutes,' said Joan. All the while she spoke, she had never taken her eyes from Lancaster's face.

Lancaster was suffering acutely. The

sweat streamed down his face, and he was looking at her with the eyes of a suffering animal. Yet it was not until the watch hand was on the hour that Joan took the bottle from the desk.

'The whole bottle is a normal dose,' said Lancaster through his teeth.

Joan drew one-fourth into the syringe.

'You must give me all, Miss Wentworth. That little quantity is useless.'

He was lying about the strength of the dose, and he knew that Joan knew. She did not answer him. He extended his arm, and she plunged the needle into the wrist. Then she corked the bottle and put it into the pocket of her uniform, having previously added the small quantity in the bottle upon the table.

The hammering at the door had begun again. But the woman waited until the spasms of pain disappeared from Lancaster's face. He rose.

'Miss Wentworth,' he began gratefully. Then, catching sight of her bruised wrists, he took her hands in his. 'Did I do that?' he cried.

'Not you, Dr. Lancaster,' answered Joan,

snatching her wrists away. 'Your enemy — our enemy, who is now worsted in his first field of battle.'

'Miss Wentworth, you see now what I am. I can't hold you to your promise. You must leave me. Who's that at the door?'

'We shall see,' answered Joan, and unlocked it.

Myers was standing outside, white with rage, and with him was Dr. Jenkins, looking uneasy and embarrassed as his eyes fell before Joan's. 'Tell her what you told me!' stammered Myers, beside himself with anger.

'Miss Wentworth,' faltered Jenkins, 'indeed you don't understand what you're doing. Dr. Lancaster — '

'Is a very sick man,' burst out the secretary. 'And it's my job to prevent him from being killed by meddlers. He picked this nurse up somewhere, and she's trying to get rid of me and have the charge of the doctor. I won't stand for it,' he added to Joan. 'I warned you twice today, and you paid no attention to me. Now you can pack up and leave the institute. Isn't that right, Doctor?' he added to Lancaster.

To Joan's stupefaction, Lancaster's old ir-
resolution had already returned, and more;
he seemed to ally himself with the secretary.
The morphine which had restored his body
had lent him its own false personality.

'Well, you see, Miss Wentworth means
well,' he said slowly, 'but she doesn't realize
certain things. You see,' he added, turning
to Joan but not meeting her eyes, 'one has
to taper off very slowly in a desperate case
like mine. I'm very far gone, and heroic
measures are useless.'

'That's right. Now tell her to go,' said
Myers.

'Yes, Miss Wentworth, I really don't believe that you can do any good here,' said
Lancaster obediently. 'It was a mistake. You
shall be paid a full month's salary. Ask Mr.
Myers to make out your check.'

'She can drive back with Dr. Jenkins
now,' suggested Myers.

'She can drive back with Dr. Jenkins,'
agreed Lancaster, and Joan saw the secretary's pale face blaze with triumph.

'And you might get me a few more
bottles from the storeroom,' whispered
Lancaster to Myers. 'I'm very shaky. I must

have enough on hand in case I wake up in the night. You understand my needs, Myers,' he continued with a catch of self-pity in his voice.

Joan did not hesitate a moment. She slipped between the two men and ran to the storeroom. With a muttered oath, Myers ran after her. Joan was just in time to slam the door in his face and lean against it inside, bracing her foot against a plank and using the whole weight of her body. She heard Myers breathe heavily as he tried to force his entrance. He dashed himself madly against it, but Joan knew that she would die rather than yield.

'Open that door!' shrieked Myers in an uncontrollable fury. 'Open at once, do you hear me?'

Joan looked hastily about her. Some instinct seemed to tell her that the case of morphine bottles was hidden under the linen pile in the near corner. By stretching out one hand without giving way in the least, she could just reach far enough to toss away the napkins. There were dozens of the tiny bottles in the packing case beneath — enough to kill a herd of oxen.

Joan heard Jenkins's protesting voice outside, and the irresolute tones of Lancaster. The matron was speaking, too. Joan did not know what they were saying to Myers, beyond the general sense of their expostulations, but she felt her will ride high above the storm of conflict.

A hammer lay on the shelf. Joan took it in her hand. 'Listen!' she cried to those outside. 'I have the morphine and I have the hammer. And I am going to break every bottle in this room — '

Lancaster cried out pitifully at her words: 'Miss Wentworth, you'll kill me if you do!'

'Unless this case passes into my possession, I am going to have the storeroom key, and I am going to take charge of Dr. Lancaster, who has employed me for that especial purpose, during this month.'

The silence of stupefaction outside was complete. Joan flung the door open boldly and stood before the group, the hammer in her hand. She saw Lancaster, with eyes bent inquiringly upon hers; the matron and Jenkins, both mute; and Myers, leaning against the opposite wall of the passage, regarding her with venomous impotence.

'Well, what do you say to that, Doctor?' he sneered.

'It isn't what Dr. Lancaster says that matters now,' answered Joan. 'It's what I say. Mrs. Fraser, please give me the storeroom key.'

The woman, looking askance at Myers, let her hand slip down toward the bunch at her side.

'The key, please,' repeated Joan, and received it. Quickly she locked the door and put the key in the pocket of her uniform.

'Now,' she said, 'I want you all to understand this situation. I am employed by Dr. Lancaster. I am under orders not to go until the month is ended. I am in charge of him. Until he's responsible for his actions, I shall remain in charge, under Dr. Jenkins. Dr. Jenkins, is it your order that Dr. Lancaster is to receive a whole dose of morphine every few hours, or the amount he has been taking?'

'Why, Miss Wentworth, I never ordered that,' protested Jenkins. 'You see, Miss Wentworth — '

'Until you do,' interposed Joan bluntly, 'I shall continue the treatment as I learned it in Dr. Lancaster's hospital at Avonmouth. And if the storeroom is opened by anyone but myself, I shall take legal action to protect Dr. Lancaster's interests.'

'Miss Wentworth,' cried Myers, 'you're making a tragedy where none exists! Nobody wants to harm the doctor. We all have one sole thought, to help him. Don't we, Doctor?' he continued, addressing Lancaster.

'You're all very kind to me,' Lancaster mumbled.

'There, you see!' said Myers, turning toward Joan again. 'There may exist differences of opinion,' he continued in a facile manner, 'and maybe I've expressed myself too forcibly. But we're all at one in wishing the doctor to get well as quickly as he can.'

He was almost fawning now, but Joan remained inflexible. She knew that if she relaxed from the nervous tension that was upholding her, she would falter.

The group dispersed. Myers followed Joan out to the veranda and stood for a long time near the door, watching her as she sat at the further end, trying to compose herself. At last he came up to her.

'See here, Miss Wentworth,' he began impetuously, 'I've come to you twice and spoken fairly to you. Maybe you see now that it would've been wiser to have met me in the same spirit. Come, now, are we to work together as friends or not?'

'I have no objection,' answered Joan. 'But my duty concerns nobody but the doctor.'

'You mean you won't cooperate with me in saving him from himself?' He looked at her with sullen challenge in his eyes.

'I do,' said Joan.

Myers thrust his hands into his pockets. 'Right!' he said. 'Three times is enough. I understand. And that's the last you'll hear from me about it.'

He went away, and Joan sat staring across the darkening hills. How had she managed to successfully fight this blind battle of hers thus far? She did not know; but whatever the hold might be that Myers had over Lancaster, she felt that Myers himself was in dread of its discovery.

Presently she saw the matron come cautiously out of the house and hurry toward her. 'How did you do it, Miss Wentworth?'

she asked in awe. 'You did what none of us would have dared to do; not me, nor Dr. Jenkins.'

'Why not?' asked Joan. 'Mrs. Fraser, of whom are you afraid? And Dr. Lancaster? It isn't that man Myers, whom the doctor could send about his business at any time when he found strength of will. Who is it?'

'Oh, Miss Wentworth, I don't know,' the matron sobbed. 'But save the doctor! Oh, do save the doctor from that man who is trying to kill him!'

5

The Fight Begins

Joan had had supper with Lancaster, and it was night, and once more the fight was raging. She had sat on the veranda with him, had talked with him, had seen the better soul of the man rise to the surface as he struggled with the morphine devil; then she had given him his half-dose again, and, as his strength revived and the agony departed, she had seen the facile, lying spirit enter into him. Now he was reposing, wrapped in his dressing gown, upon his bed, and she sat at his side, at grips with the devil in him that clamored for its victim's body, that it might possess it entirely, as surely an evil as any spirit of evil, though its shrine was a little glass bottle holding a few drops of fluid.

She was fighting for the better Lancaster again, and he was writhing in torment and pleading with her to go, to leave him to his fate, since the suffering was intolerable and subjection preferable. There was an hour of hideous battle, but somehow Joan managed to keep him quiet till midnight. And, seated beside him, watching him, she came to the conclusion that his was one of those strange cases of double personality of which she had read in medical books. It was impossible to reconcile this Lancaster in any way with the man whom she had seen momentarily at the hospital, and with the tyrant of the operating room. For that man was essentially base and ignoble, and this man was honor and truth when the morphine fiend retired, baffled for a space; and under that pitiful load of shame she sensed the cleanness of the man's soul and its integrity.

Somehow she held this devil at bay until midnight. And then, with a second victory, to his credit, he stretched out his arm for the hypodermic. Then Joan saw the look of contentment come into his face, heard the satisfied sigh — and there was the old Lancaster before her; shifty, furtive, and false. No, not altogether, for something of that victory remained with him, the promise of renewed manhood; the morphine devil was losing its grip. Ground had been won. It should never be ceded. Joan swore that as she watched by the bedside.

'Dr. Lancaster, you've promised me to sleep till six,' she said. 'Can I trust you?'

'How can you doubt my word, Miss Wentworth?' asked Lancaster with an affectation of surprise. 'Of course you can. You know, I'm not a regular user of drugs. I've been overworked and I took morphine to make me sleep, and somehow it got hold of me. I think I must be unusually susceptible to the drug.'

The old lie of the stupid drug devil! But Joan had the storeroom key, and she knew that it would require a hammer or ax to break down the strong door. And she would wake and hear him, and fight again as she had fought that morning.

'Then I'm going to bed till six,' she said.

'But Miss Wentworth,' he protested, 'six hours is an impossibly long period. Every three hours is my time, and now that I'm on half-doses — you remember what Jenkins said this morning. You must go slowly with a confirmed drug user like myself ... ' He added suddenly: 'Stop! Don't listen to me! You can trust me, Miss Wentworth. I'm going to fight this out, and — '

'You're winning,' answered Joan, bending over him. 'Don't forget that. Say 'I'm winning' whenever the pain seems uncontrollable and your will seems gone. It won't last long. Dr. Lancaster, you are your own self at this moment, and nothing can harm you. Fight the good fight!'

He caught her hand and carried it to his lips. 'Miss Wentworth, you are my good angel!' he cried. 'I secured the services of an angel unawares,' he added, looking at her with that pathetic humor which went straight to her heart. 'I want to win for your sake. But why are you taking so much trouble for a worthless old fellow like me?'

'Don't flatter yourself that it's all for you, Dr. Lancaster. Perhaps I may want to save the most distinguished surgeon in the south.'

At her words he started and stared at her, and then fell back upon the pillow, hiding his face. Joan turned away. Again she had touched some hidden spring of memory; what it was she could not know, but it was evident that she had wounded him to the quick. Perhaps it was the contrast between the office he held and the man he had become. Perhaps it was the knowledge of his secret bondage which had broken him down at last and driven him back to the institute, and Myers.

'Miss Wentworth, I want you to lock my door and take away the key,' he said. 'I may have a secret supply somewhere.'

'I don't think you have,' answered Joan. 'You have none in this room, have you?'

'No.'

'I believe that. And anyway, I'm going to trust you. That is part of your fight. I am going to trust you till six.'

He said good night in a low tone and turned away. Joan went up to her room. She lay down, but did not undress. She admitted that she was afraid, and nothing but Lancaster's desperate need of her would have kept her an hour longer in the institute. But she was exhausted from the day, and soon she was asleep.

But she slept that sleep which brings no recreation for the jaded body or the overwrought mind. All the while she was back with Lancaster in his room below, in spirit. She knew that, as he had said, the drug bondage was only the climax of his difficulties.

What had there been that had wrecked the man? Jenkins had hinted at stolen funds. Of one thing she was sure: Lancaster, sunken as he was, was incapable of such dishonesty. In her sleep, her brain went on puzzling over the problem. Only her body was quiescent, and it lay wearily in the bed like some chained captive.

But suddenly, the urgent summons of the brain shook from it the trammels of sleep. Joan listened intently, awake upon the instant, as some wild creature of the woods that senses danger. Somebody was coming along the corridor.

The footfalls were so soft and stealthy that she might have thought she was dreaming, but for the sense of imminent danger, the knowledge of some malevolent design. The steps stopped and began again, the merest touches of sound against the silence of night, the lightest patter of bare feet outside the door.

Then the door began to open.

There was no moon, and the faint starlight outside only seemed to render darker the obscurity within. Yet through the darkness Joan knew that a hand lay on the door jamb, and that a figure watched her across the room.

She leaped from her bed. 'Who's there?' she called in tones that seemed to shock the silence.

She could see nothing now, and she dared not turn aside to light her lamp. She knew that the figure was crouching somewhere. She heard the softest breathing, but could not locate it in the room. She felt the atmosphere of evil that surrounded her. She started to cross the room, groping, with arms outstretched. Then she found the intruder and flung herself upon it. Her left hand closed about a wrist, supple and strong. Her right hand held another hand. They wrestled in the darkness, their bodies tense but motionless, only the hands and wrist muscles at strife. Not a sound came from their lips.

Joan thought it was a woman's hands she held. Her fingers sought the menace in the closed fists. The left hand of the intruder was empty, but in the right was a jagged piece of a broken tumbler that tinkled to the floor.

As it fell, the intruder leaped at her as if strung upon wires. Joan saw, very dimly, the face of Mrs. Dana. She was in her night-dress, with her feet bare, and the ferocity of her attack seemed atrocious in contrast with the expressionless, mask-like features. Only the eyes seemed alive, and they burned with implacable hatred, as if they meditated revenge for all the accumulation of a life's wrongs.

The woman bore Joan backward. The lamp fell crashing to the floor in a debacle of splintered glass. A chair was overturned. Mrs. Dana's hands sought Joan's throat, and they struggled in the darkness, crashing here and there, upsetting the water pitcher, smashing into the swinging door.

Underneath her Joan heard Mrs. Fraser moving and doors opening. There were steps on the stairs.

For a few moments Joan felt no match for the onset of the madwoman. But Mrs. Dana's impulse was soon exhausted. Joan got her arms about her body, pressing her arms to her sides. Mrs. Dana suddenly became passive, and the lights in her eyes seemed to go out like extinguished candles as her brain clouded. Joan got her into the corridor. At the further end a little lamp was burning.

Mrs. Dana went with her quietly, walking like a mechanical figure. At the head of the stairs appeared the matron, wearing a white wrapper. Behind her Joan saw the startled faces of Myers and Lancaster.

Joan let Mrs. Dana into her room, and Mrs. Fraser came at her heels, breathing hard in terror. 'Did she hurt you?' she gasped. 'How did she get out? Who let her out? I should have told you she was dangerous, but I never dreamed that she could pick that lock. Did she — did she try to harm you?'

'She had a piece of glass,' said Joan, 'but I took it away from her.'

'There was no glass in her room last evening,' said the matron with conviction.

Lancaster was approaching. Joan was astounded to see the look of anger on his face. 'Who opened that door?' he shouted.

'It's all right now, Dr. Lancaster,' came the matron's voice from within.

But Lancaster was shaking with excitement. He swung round upon Myers. 'You are responsible for this!' he cried. 'You know my one point that has to be carried out. I told you to have a bolt put on the door after she got out before.'

'Now, now, Doctor, don't excite yourself,' said the secretary soothingly. 'You're a sick man, you know. It was unfortunate, but I'll see it doesn't happen again.'

Lancaster seemed beside himself with fury; far more angry, indeed, than the situation appeared to warrant. 'She might have killed Miss Wentworth!' he stormed. 'I've stood enough from you without this. I've suffered you, God knows, until you've sapped my strength and crushed me under your feet, and made me less of a man than the meanest drunkard in Millville, but now it's ended. Get out of my sight! Leave the institute tomorrow!'

Myers seemed stricken with fear and agitation. 'Why, Doctor,' he protested, 'you don't know what you're talking about. That nurse's treatment has upset your nerves. It's your way to hire people when you feel fine and then discharge them when you're not well. You'll think better of it in the morning. I'm not going any more than Miss Wentworth did.'

Lancaster's face was twisted. He raised his fist as if to strike Myers. Joan saw the secretary recoil, and she divined that the man was a physical coward.

'I tell you I've done with you!' cried Lancaster. 'My mind's made up. Go ahead and do your worst.'

'Say,' shouted Myers, 'am I responsible if that woman got out of her room? What's the sense of picking on me? Didn't you hire a nurse to take care of your patients? Isn't Mrs. Dana a patient? Now there's been enough said, I reckon. You know what I mean, Doctor. Better go back to your room and forget what you've said tonight.'

'If ever I see your face after tonight, by God, I'll kill you!' shouted Lancaster.

Myers slunk away toward the stairs. 'Oh, all right, all right,' he answered. 'I reckon you'll be sorry tomorrow. But I'll hold you to what you've said. I won't see that nurse bust up my work here.'

He scowled fearfully at Joan as he went down the stairs, a grotesque, almost deformed figure in his loose pajamas. But Joan hardly heeded the man. She did not know the cause of Lancaster's sudden outbreak of rage, but she knew that it was part of the whole dreadful problem, and that in fighting Lancaster's driving devil she was at work upon the darkest corner of the dark mystery.

'I think, Dr. Lancaster, you had better go and lie down again,' she told him. 'No harm has been done, but I'm very sorry you were awakened.'

He was leaning against the wall, looking at her with a strange expression upon his face. He breathed quickly, like a man in uncontrollable agitation. Just then the matron came out of Mrs. Dana's room.

'How did it happen, Mrs. Fraser?' asked Lancaster.

The matron snapped the key in the lock before answering. 'I don't know, Dr. Lancaster,' she answered. 'The lock's all right. It couldn't have been picked. And I swear I locked it last night. Somebody must have let her out.'

'That hound!' began Lancaster, but Joan interposed.

'She may have found a key,' she said.

The matron shook her head. 'No key would fit that lock except this one,' she answered.

'Why should anyone tamper with that lock?' Lancaster muttered. Suddenly he broke down and covered his face with his hands. His shoulders shook convulsively. Joan put her hand on his arm.

'Dr. Lancaster, you must go back to your room now,' she said. 'It was nothing, and it's all over.'

He raised his face. 'Yes, you're right, Miss Wentworth,' he answered simply.

The matron had slipped away down the stairs. The secretary was pacing his room, loudly slamming open lids of trunks and bureau drawers. Joan divined that it was his threat of leaving, designed to reach Lancaster's ears. At the door of the doctor's room Lancaster hesitated. His furious rage had burned itself away, leaving him in a reaction of fear and weakness. The hands of the clock in the hall pointed to five. Joan dared not leave Lancaster alone until six.

But, as if he understood her thoughts, he said: 'Miss Wentworth, if you'll stay with me till six, it would help me to master myself. It is not the fear of yielding to morphine; it's my thoughts. If you know how one's life comes crowding upon one in the darkness — '

'I'll stay with you,' said Joan.

'Let's wait on the veranda,' said Lancaster. 'The air is stifling in this house. Put on a wrap and I'll wait for you there.'

Joan ran upstairs and slipped on her cloak. When she got back, Lancaster had not moved from the door. The secretary was packing noisily in his room. They went outside together, closing the front door behind them, as if to shut in the evil influences of the place. There was a hint of morning in the air, in its freshness, in the paling of the night above the eastern mountains. There was the fresh night-scent of the pines, and all the stillness of that hour which seems to hold nature entranced between her sleep and her awakening.

Lancaster led the way toward the chairs at the end of the veranda and wiped the dew from them with his handkerchief. 'When you came here,' he said as they sat down, 'when on the impulse I asked you to come here, I never dreamed that my impulse was the prompting of my good angel.'

'You said I was your good angel,' said Joan lightly.

'It was more than chance,' said Lancaster seriously. 'It was the happiest thing that has ever happened to me.'

'Dr. Lancaster, I'm only too glad to have had the opportunity of being of service. It's what every nurse would have wished.'

'No,' he corrected her. 'You've brought more than service to the institute. Do you know what you've brought? Hope!'

She could hardly restrain her tears, so deeply was she moved. She put her hand upon his. 'Dr. Lancaster, it must never leave you again,' she answered. 'Lift up your eyes and look at the hills. How can one help but hope? Hope lies all about you.'

'When a man lives in darkness,' said Lancaster gravely, 'he can't lift up his eyes. I was broken long before I became a victim of that damnable drug. I fell into the hands of unscrupulous men. I had nothing to live for. I dwelled in shadows, hardly knowing the dream from the reality, and all the men and women about me seemed like shadows until you came. I could endure my life only because of its unreality; it was like a dream, a nightmare which, I know, couldn't last forever.'

She did not answer, and he remained silent for a long time.

It began to lighten. Streaks of saffron appeared against the tops of the hills. Broad swaths of mist were rolling down the valleys. A bird awoke and called; another answered.

'But this is hope,' said Lancaster, taking Joan's hand. 'You've brought it to me, and I'm never going to lose it again. I'm going to win my fight against the drug, and then I'm going to regain everything else that I've lost.'

He seemed upon the verge of a revelation, but he said no more. And now the day was dawning. It became light: the rim of the sun appeared suddenly over the mountain horizon, the mists went rolling upward, and the whole land was revealed in sunlight.

The hall clock struck six. Joan looked at Lancaster. His face was twisted with pain, his lips bloodless from compression. 'You've made a splendid fight, Dr. Lancaster,' she said. 'Now you shall have your hypodermic.'

He rose up eagerly, and she could see the terrific strain that he was undergoing in the trembling of his limbs, the eager look in his eyes. They went back into the house. A light still burned in the secretary's room, but no sound came from it.

At the door of Lancaster's room they stopped. 'Miss Wentworth,' he said, 'I have something to say and something to promise. I'm not going to take that dose. Tonight, perhaps, but not now. If I take it and free my body from its suffering, I lose my soul again. I lose the hope you've given me. And I want to give you this.'

He handed her a little bottle of morphine, three-quarters full.

'It's the bottle you took from the drawer of my desk yesterday,' he said. 'I stole it from your pocket when you leaned over me last night and told me I was winning. I was a thief, but I'm a penitent one, and I restore it intact.'

'No, Dr. Lancaster,' answered Joan, smiling as she took the bottle from him. 'That has no bearing upon your character; it was a symptom of your disease.'

'Well, I didn't take any,' said Lancaster

with a transient flash of humor lighting up his face. 'I had the hardest conceivable battle over that bottle. I set it up before me and held my right hand back with my left, and I said, 'I am winning, in Joan Wentworth's name.' And at last the drug devil was beaten. And no more morphine until tonight.'

'Dr. Lancaster, you've been brave and wonderful!' cried Joan, profoundly stirred. 'Remember that! One of the bravest men I've ever known. Never tell me again that you've lost your willpower. We're winning fast.'

He placed his hands upon her shoulders and stood looking at her. Upon his face was an expression of indulgence, as if he were considering her enthusiasm in the light of his experience of life — so much deeper than hers; so much the more profound. Then the look passed; the years seemed to fall from him, and strength came into his face. 'God bless you, my dear,' he said, and bent to kiss her forehead.

She turned and ran upstairs. Her heart was singing in her breast. The flood of sunlight that came through the eastern windows, illuminating the dusty interior of the old building, seemed like a spiritual light, flaming into this dark place where shadows had dwelled so long. She went into her room and dressed for the day. She had never felt so happy before. And now the life in Avonmouth had become as dim as a dream, and she cared no longer whether she returned or not.

A charge had been granted to her; a man's life into her keeping. That trust she meant to fulfill. She had saved Lancaster, and she would outwit Myers and remove the only obstacle to Lancaster's recovery. She knew the man incited the doctor to drug himself.

As she stood at her window, Joan heard footsteps on the path below. Looking down, she saw the secretary leaving the house, carrying a suitcase. Her heart almost stood still. Surely Myers had not acknowledged defeat and taken Lancaster at his word? Surely he did not mean to go without another struggle? She watched him cross the grass beside the chicken coop to where the weed-grown path joined the winding road. He was outside the grounds of the institute now, and he was still going in the direction of the station. He disappeared behind the hedges, appeared again a long way off, and then vanished finally. He was gone, and the air seemed the sweeter, the day more glorious.

Joan almost danced downstairs to the dining room. Lancaster was at the table waiting for her. 'Mr. Myers has gone away!' she cried. 'Dr. Lancaster, your evil spirit has departed, suitcase and all.'

Lancaster looked at her gravely. 'I know,' he said.

'Did he come to you? Did you discharge him?'

'He did not come to me. He did not tell the matron he was going. It looks bad.'

'No,' said Joan firmly, struggling against her conviction. 'He was afraid. You'll never see him again.'

'You know what the Bible says about the unclean spirit who leaves a man and returns with seven others when he finds his home swept and garnished?'

'Dr. Lancaster, he has no hold on you. He can do nothing, and he'll never dare return.'

'Well, my dear, we have a respite, at all events,' Lancaster answered. 'So let's eat our breakfast, and afterward I'll take you for a ramble through the woods. We'll hold the fort together until evening.'

⋆ ⋆ ⋆

By the next morning there was no doubt that victory had been won. There was color in Lancaster's face, a lightness to his step, and, best of all, he was psychically whole. The drug devil still clung to the nervous refuges of its physical domain — the hands still trembled, and the man started at sounds; but the shifty, furtive, lying spirit had taken its departure.

Lancaster had gone through the worst of his ordeal; and yet certain features of his illness were puzzling to both of them. The symptoms of morphine poisoning, elusive and protean as they are, seemed in this case irreconcilable with those that are classically accepted. There was Lancaster's complete prostration on the morning when Joan discovered the nature of his illness. He told her afterward that he had been conscious all the time, but physically inert, as if paralyzed. That did not point to morphine poisoning. And a certain lethargy remained one of the last symptoms of the case.

The intimacy of the sickroom, born of their struggle, had become the most natural thing to both of them. The passing of Myers had wrought an extraordinary change in the atmosphere of the institution. And somehow the news of Lancaster's recovery had spread into Millville. Joan inferred that even the country people had boycotted the institute, but now two mothers brought their babies to Lancaster, and it was amazing and delightful to Joan to see the doctor's transformation, with his jolliness and tenderness toward the children.

'I'm using my respite,' he said whimsically. 'I want to get well to face my harder battle.'

'This is no respite,' answered Joan. 'You're free now, Dr. Lancaster; it's only a habit of thought that holds you.'

He shook his head, and at the moment she thought that he intended to confide in her. But he said nothing, and she was content that he should remain silent until he chose to speak. If ever.

There ensued three wonderful days after the secretary's departure, always to remain clear in Joan's memory. They were three days of uninterrupted recovery. After the second, no more morphine was given. The fight was won; there was no questioning that.

'I suppose you'll have to return to Avonmouth soon,' Joan suggested.

The doctor turned a startled look on her. 'Yes — soon,' he said, and fell into a gloomy meditation from which she could not arouse him.

That afternoon a telephone message came from Thompson, a hill village fifteen miles distant. A farm hand had been crushed by a falling tree; would Lancaster come at once and see if anything could be done for him?

'Would you like to come with me?' he asked Joan.

'If I can be of help.'

'Of course you can — the greatest help. I shall need you badly, perhaps to administer an anesthetic,' he answered.

Lancaster telephoned to Jenkins for the buggy, and half an hour later they were driving along the country road into the heart of the mountains.

They traveled for the most part in silence; Lancaster's thoughts were occupied with his prospective case, and Joan was content to sit quietly at his side and watch the changing panorama of the land she loved and knew so well. She felt at home in these mountains, which she had seen afar off from girlhood and never explored. They had stood in her mind unconsciously as a symbol of the struggle of life and its conquest; and she was thinking vaguely that as she had come to them at last, so her life, too, had opened out and revealed difficult places.

The road ascended continuously until at last, when the sun was low down in the sky, they entered Thompson, a tiny settlement in the very heart of the mountain peaks.

6

The Engagement

It was a serious case, and the patient was already comatose. The tree had fallen across the chest, crushing it and driving a rib into a lung. An immediate operation offered the only hope, and the doctor decided to perform it in the cabin.

Joan, having bundled out the family and the neighbors, administered the ether. She had never been greatly impressed by the legend of the skilled surgeon with the wonderful touch; her first operation at Avonmouth had seemed to her like a sort of glorified plumbing, and the leisurely manner of the surgeons had reduced the art to a science in her estimation. Now she revised her opinion as, seated at the patient's head, she watched Lancaster working within a compass of fractional inches, where a slip would have been deadly. His fingers, which had trembled as he held the reins, were as steady as the steel instruments he held; his deftness and precision were amazing; and when at last the operation was ended, and the patient's recovery announced as probable, she could not conceal her enthusiasm.

They were to remain at the cabin overnight in case of a change for the worse, returning to the institute in the morning. After a scrappy meal, they had wandered to the end of the village toward a patch of woodland that was encroaching on the tiny settlement. The long summer twilight still held the land, although the mountain tops were already vague and shadowy. They stood looking down toward the level country under them.

'I think you're the most wonderful surgeon in the world,' said Joan. 'And you see, I didn't faint this time,' she added.

'Faint? Why should you faint?' asked Lancaster, looking at her with a puzzled expression.

'You seemed to regard my weakness in the operating room as a sign of my incapacity,' she replied, a little chagrined that he should have dismissed the matter from his mind.

Lancaster looked at her with that strange glance which seemed always designed to hide his thoughts. Then his face softened. 'Joan, do you know that I owe everything on earth to you, my dear?' he asked. And he took her in his arms and kissed her. 'That's what you mean to me,' he said. 'I can't lose you; I want you to fill the life that you've given back to me.'

At the touch of his lips on hers, Joan knew that in truth she loved him. All that she had heard of the man's past — his dissolute life, the talk of Avonmouth — was forgotten. She only knew that she loved him, not with the wild passion of which she had heard, but with a quiet and abiding fondness, none the weaker for its qualities of calmness; and it was the most natural thing in the world that she, who had given him life again, should give her own life also to this wonderful, strong man who had risen above his wrongs and driven the besetting devils from him by valorous strength. Her heart was lifted up. Serene and trusting, she returned his kiss.

'I love you, too,' she answered. 'Nothing of the past shall ever come between us.'

They were at the verge of the forest, upon a height that overlooked Millville and Lancaster — hill villages, but now outspread in the shadowy plain beneath them. A dozen counties could be dimly discerned from that spot by daylight. Far in the distance were the coastal lands, nearer the cultivated belt, nearer still the little farms, and the matchless mountains all about them. It was their home country — both of them were thinking that the smell of the rich soil was in their nostrils, and in their hearts the sense of home.

'Joan, can a man begin to build up his life again at thirty-eight, after he's missed everything?' asked Lancaster after a long silence.

'You've proved that he can,' she answered. 'But you haven't missed everything, my dear. You are a very great man, and a man with great work to do in the world. Many men have gone along the path you took, but few have found the strength to turn back as you have done.'

'Joan, I want to tell you something. I was engaged to be married once years ago. She ran away on the evening before our

131

marriage day. It was the beginning of my downfall. I thought I loved her.'

His face was haggard. Divining his distress, Joan slipped her hand into his.

'Joan, dearest,' said Lancaster after a pause, 'I have often thought that someday I'd tell you all the wretched story of my past. But I've been thinking differently today. I was entrapped by an unscrupulous man who robbed me of everything that made my life worth living. But there's nothing that would make me afraid to look fellow men in the face. It is myself who I have shamed and humiliated. Joan, I want to say nothing; not because I would keep anything from you, but because I want to start my life anew. I shall never go back to the institute.'

'You mean — '

'Never. I shall not return tomorrow. I want you to come to the southwest with me, Joan, my dear. We'll drive across the hills to Carroll's and catch the through train there. I'll begin the new life you've given me. Will you leave everything for my sake, Joan? Is it too hard a request?'

'No, it's not,' she answered. 'But it's not right for you.'

'It's right for me to leave a living death behind me.'

'No, dear. It's running away. You spoke to me of some harder fight to be fought.'

'With nothing to win, Joan — nothing. When I leave Lancaster, no human being will miss or regret me.'

'There's your work at Avonmouth. There's the hospital you've made famous throughout the United States. Your work is there, not in some obscure place where it would be of less use to the world and no example. Besides, consider that if you become famous again, as you must, you'll be discovered. And one can never leave his past behind him. That follows everywhere.'

'Yes, that's true,' muttered Lancaster, staring out over the darkening hills. 'Well, I leave it to you, my dear; but to go back to fight a futile battle seems to me now something unendurable.'

'You must go back to the institute, and then to Avonmouth, and meet your enemies, John,' she said. 'I shall be at your side. Nothing will make me afraid or weaken my love for you.'

His face twitched. 'Not if I tell you

things which prove me worthless of your love?' he asked. 'Not if you find I'm an outcast man who deserves his misfortunes?'

She only smiled at him. 'I won't judge you by your words,' she said, 'nor yet by other men's opinions, but by my knowledge of you.'

'Then I'll tell you everything,' he answered, drawing Joan's hand into his. 'Everything, but not here. Here I shall keep the peace of the hills within my heart, and you.'

So they strolled back toward the cabin, and Joan's drab-colored life was transmuted in this, her first love, to gold. She lived in her lover; she trusted wholly in him who had brought love to her, not like a conquering god, but in the simplest guise, making it the unfolding of her own loving nature. She gave her youth, her innocence, as love's price, and thought the exchange her profit. There was never such peacefulness in any place as there that evening, and in Joan's heart was abounding peace likewise.

When they reached the cabin, the patient was better. Lancaster spent the evening giving detailed instructions to the man's wife. 'I shall do my best to come again if I'm needed,' he said, 'but I can't promise. I may be called to Avonmouth at any moment. Keep him quiet, for heaven's sake keep him absolutely motionless for a week, and then let him sit up if he wants to. And nothing to eat but the schedule I'm making out for you.'

Afterwards, Joan told Lancaster that she wished to stay for a few days to take care of the man. But he would not hear of it. 'These hill people never die,' he said. 'He'll be up and about before the week is over.'

'But the diet?'

'They'll feed him on soda biscuits as soon as he's well enough to eat anything. Fortunately he won't be able to eat for a week, so he won't come to any harm. I shall send Jenkins over two or three times to report progress.'

Joan's room was a tiny place under the eaves. She spent a sleepless but content night there, thinking over the happiness that had come to her. It was strange and wonderful to lie awake under the same roof that sheltered Lancaster and to reflect how soon their lives would flow together calmly in their own country. She could not have wished any other fate in life. With her limited experience, it seemed ideal that after the years of stress in Avonmouth, she should be returning, almost to her own home, a wife. She had puzzled sometimes over Lancaster's long residences in the place that bore his name. But she dreamed of the time when he would give up his work at Avonmouth and retire to a new institute, a spacious home where they could fill their wards with the country people, where her life's vocation and her life's happiness would be united.

At last she fell asleep, and when she awoke Lancaster was tapping at her door. 'Time to get up, Joan!' he called cheerfully.

She sprang out of bed. 'How is the patient?' she asked.

'Doing nicely and wants to go to work,' said Lancaster, laughing.

Joan dressed in a hurry and ran downstairs. Lancaster was waiting on the porch. She raised her face for his kiss, already natural to her, already the happy fulfillment of her innocent dreams of love. Then arm in arm they strolled out into the sunlight.

The glorious light lay on every hill; it swept the land in a torrent of golden brightness. In that light all the shadows of the past seemed to shrivel away.

'We're going back to the institute this morning, Joan,' said Lancaster.

She nodded happily. 'I'm ashamed to feel so gay when you're unhappy,' she said.

'I'm not unhappy, Joan,' he answered. 'I thought over everything last night, and I see now that you were right. I shall go back. I shall regain what I've lost, and I shall face my enemies and beat them.'

At ten o'clock the horse was harnessed and the drive back began. At first Joan, seated at her lover's side, breathed in the mountain air, the sense of freedom, the scent of the pines, the joy of the sunlight. Then the peaks began to tower above them. The duller valley air struck something from her joy, but not too much for her to dream. She looked fondly at Lancaster, who drew her hand into his.

'I'm going back to win,' he said again.

Later the sun went into clouds. The air grew moister, the hills enclosed them, and the familiar landmarks began to reappear.

And now something of Lancaster's despondency of the evening before came over Joan. As if sensing her mood, he reiterated: 'I am going back to fight and win, my dear.'

But when the institute came into sight at last, the long, gaunt building cast its chill over Joan's heart. In contrast with the mountain village, Lancaster was depressing and lonely. And Joan was conscious of one gripping fear. Suppose Myers had returned! She understood now how Lancaster had felt the evening before when he said he would never go back. It was like plunging out of the sunlight into a dark mountain pool.

The matron came forward as the buggy stopped. Joan looked at her in terror. But her face was placid enough, and she was able to read in it the secretary's continued absence.

'Dr. Lancaster, there was a telephone message for you a few minutes ago from Avonmouth,' she said.

Lancaster leaped from the buggy and helped Joan down. 'I'll be with you in a few moments,' he said, throwing the reins over the hitching post.

He went into the house. His step was

firm, his demeanor unruffled; the matron, who followed him, seemed undisturbed. But already everything was changed. The black shadow of Myers seemed to loom up until it overspread the institute again. Joan paced the porch in fear which gathered strength each moment that Lancaster failed to return. When at last she saw him coming, her suspense was unbearable. She looked at him in mute fear as he laid his hand caressingly upon her shoulder.

'I have to go to Avonmouth at once,' he said. 'I have no choice in the matter. It's a patient who must undergo an operation — my operation — within twelve hours. It's fortunate that we have the buggy, because I shall just have time to catch the afternoon train and get into Avonmouth by midnight.' Then he looked at her white face and read the fear in it. 'If you tell me to stay, I'll stay,' he said.

'And the patient?' whispered Joan.

'Will die. No, of course I shall go. Nothing could keep me from going, not even you, my dear. But you wouldn't have me stay.'

'Yes, of course you must go. But I'm

afraid,' said Joan. 'I'm afraid of Myers.'

He started as if he, too, had been thinking of the secretary. 'But the man can't harm me, dear,' he said.

'The message came from him!' cried Joan in fear.

Lancaster looked away. But when she repeated the question he answered, 'No.'

'He's at Avonmouth — is he not there?' she asked.

'Well, Joan, I think he is,' said Lancaster reluctantly. 'But he may not be. I only know that the message was not from him.'

'It was from the hospital? Not from MacPherson?'

'It was from a man connected with the hospital,' said Lancaster. 'But it wasn't from MacPherson or Myers, and it didn't mention Myers's name. Why, my dear, you mustn't give way to nerves now that I'm losing mine. It's a simple request for me to operate tomorrow.'

She pulled herself together. 'Of course you must go, John,' she said again. She put her arms about his neck. 'Dear, if you should see that man, you won't fall into any trap that he may set for you?' she asked.

'You're so strong; you won't let him trample on you? You are yourself again, and you'll remain so for my sake?'

'Never fear!' he answered cheerfully. 'I'm not going to take morphine again. Why, I shall have none with me, my dear Joan, and I should have no opportunity to buy any, even if I wanted to. I shall operate perhaps as soon as I reach the hospital, and return on the morning train. I may not even go to my house at all.'

'I'm not afraid that you'll take morphine,' said Joan. 'But you won't see Myers?'

'Not if I can help it. He can't come to the hospital, and I don't think he would dare to lie in wait for me at the station. If he does, he'll find me a tough customer to kidnap in broad daylight. There, my dear, be calm and sensible, and when I return I shall tell you everything you need to know.'

He kissed her and hurried in to pack his suitcase. He came out in a few moments and placed it in the buggy. 'Goodbye, dearest Joan,' he said. 'And please don't hint at our engagement to Mrs. Fraser while I'm gone. I have a very special reason for asking this of you.'

She shook her head and laughed, and returned his kiss; but all the while, her heart grew heavier. And long after the buggy had disappeared from sight, she stood upon the porch looking after it.

That night was sleepless like the last, but all the joy that had filled Joan's heart in the hill cabin was gone. She lay awake, listening to the rain that pattered on the roof, thinking and wondering. How strange her life had become, and how far away the old landmarks were! She had fought for a man's soul in darkness and snatched it into light, and now the darkness seemed to be closing about her again. And she could only hope and wait through endless hours.

In vain she tried to tell herself that it was only an ordinary summons. On the face of it the call was natural, but Joan's instinct told her that there was more behind it. Myers had not surrendered his prey as easily as it had seemed. And Lancaster had been evasive — to spare her, perhaps. Her task now was only to wait.

She tried to follow Lancaster in her mind; to picture him at the various stages of his journey, now in the train and now at

Avonmouth. Then she fell asleep for a few minutes, awakening to find that the same process had been going on in her dreams.

At eight she rose. She imagined that he must have finished the operation some time before and be at the station, or on his way there; but her soul could not go out to his across the distance, and their communion seemed to be cut short by the same impenetrable darkness.

Dressing, Joan was conscious of a stronger presentiment of approaching evil which she could not shake away. It was a gloomy day, and the rain came down in torrents. At about eleven o'clock Dr. Jenkins arrived in his buggy, and inquired for Lancaster. He seemed surprised to learn that he had gone to Avonmouth.

He was preparing to return, but Joan felt the need of speech with him. She did not mean to cross-examine him; she only wanted to shake off the feeling that Lancaster had passed out of her reach by speaking to one of his associates. She hardly knew the purpose of her accosting Jenkins until she saw the look of concern upon his face.

'Miss Wentworth, you aren't well!' he exclaimed. 'You've been overdoing it.'

'No, Dr. Jenkins. But Dr. Lancaster has gone into Avonmouth — '

'Yes, Miss Wentworth. But he won't come to any harm there, thanks to you. You've taught me a thing or two about morphine patients, Miss Wentworth,' he went on, in his polite, complimentary fashion. 'I never saw anyone get well as fast as Dr. Lancaster, nor any nurse who could handle a situation like you did.'

'Yes, but it was not really morphine, you know,' said Joan, and then she almost gaped in astonishment. What had she said? Why had she said it?

Dr. Jenkins was staring at her, too. 'Not morphine, you say, Miss Wentworth?' he stammered.

'I mean, the symptoms weren't those of morphine poisoning.'

'Oh, well, Miss Wentworth, everybody takes it in a different way. Yes, I reckon it was morphine, right enough. They wouldn't put the wrong label on the bottles. You certainly did set things humming,' he added, laughing and raising his hat.

'Wait a moment, Dr. Jenkins,' persisted Joan. 'I'm so anxious about the doctor. He ought not to have gone; he was in no condition to go. And yet a man's life is at stake.'

The doctor's face became at once impenetrable. He seemed to be on his guard against her, and to know more than she, Dr. Lancaster's fiancée, knew. It was humiliating and ironic. But Joan saw that to question him, even if she had been so minded, was useless.

The hours of afternoon were leaden ones. Through the lowering western clouds, the sun, emerging for a moment, streaked the west with angry crimson splashes. Lancaster must be nearly home. But it was no use waiting there, where Joan's fears grew from moment to moment. She went into the building and saw the matron standing within her door. Suddenly she sensed the reflection of her own fears in Mrs. Fraser's heart. She knew the woman was doing nothing as she stood there; was waiting, like herself, and in the same manner hoping against hope for the doctor's safe return.

Impulsively Joan entered the room. She

could keep silenct no longer. She broke down, sobbing distractedly. 'I'm afraid something has happened to the doctor,' she wept.

'Now you sit down in that chair, Miss Wentworth,' said Mrs. Fraser kindly. 'It's been a trying day. But Dr. Lancaster will be home in an hour, and there's no use becoming anxious about him. Heavens, if we got anxious before we had cause, what should we do?'

'I know,' sobbed Joan. 'But I can't bear waiting. I know something has happened to him.'

'Now, my dear, you are all worked up about him,' Mrs. Fraser said. 'He won't come to any harm. Not when he went straight to his own hospital.'

But she spoke without conviction. Joan's hysterical mood was infecting her, increasing her own fears and forebodings.

'I reckon you know, Miss Wentworth, how much Dr. Jenkins and I feel we owe to you for taking care of the doctor,' the matron continued, seating herself at Joan's side. 'No harm can come to him with you watching and praying for him.'

Joan looked up at her with a troubled face. 'Mrs. Fraser, I'm so much at a loss,' she said. 'You and Dr. Jenkins have known Dr. Lancaster so long, and I'm a stranger here. I'm like a child in comparison to you, so far as knowledge of Dr. Lancaster is concerned. I have been fighting his physical troubles, but I don't know about his mental ones. That puts me at a loss. How can I know that Dr. Lancaster's enemies aren't waiting for him, or haven't hurt him?'

The matron placed her hand on Joan's knee. 'Why, my dear, Dr. Lancaster has no enemies,' she said. 'How could such a splendid man have enemies? Of course, there are troubles, but who hasn't had them? And it may be there's things that Dr. Jenkins and I don't know. I've thought there might be. But we've only been here three years, and that was long after the doctor's troubles began. And, of course, we never listened to the village gossip. But, oh! Miss Wentworth, you can't imagine the sorrow in our hearts when we saw that splendid man giving way to his habit and letting it creep over him little by little and gain the mastery.

'At first, when I came here, it was only at certain times that he'd take the morphine; and then he'd have terrible outbursts of rage, and it was all that we could do to control him. I used to think that his mind would go, especially when he'd have these fits after he came back from Avonmouth. But after that, the hoodoo got him. That's when I was afraid.'

'The hoodoo?' inquired Joan.

'Miss Wentworth, the devil who was at him so long got hold of him once or twice. I've seen him come back from Avonmouth a different man. That's when I've been afraid. Because the devil that can kill the body isn't much of a devil, but when he kills the soul there's no help but prayer. When he's in the dreadful moods, he's another man — a wicked man, Miss Wentworth; and I'd shoot him then, if he tried to harm me or any of mine, and I wouldn't think I'd killed Dr. Lancaster. It all began after they accused him of stealing the trust funds.'

'It is not true,' said Joan.

'I'm sure it isn't. But you see, old Dr. Lancaster didn't leave the charge of the fund to his son; he left it in the care of the trustees. And there were complications about the hospital at Avonmouth. And, then, after the doctor's bride ran away on the eve of their marriage, it changed his nature completely.'

'I've heard about that,' said Joan quietly. 'But we mustn't discuss it in the doctor's absence.'

'Why, everybody knows about it, Miss Wentworth. Before it happened, they say the doctor was the most respected man in Lancaster. He'd been born here, you know, on the plantation down in the valley Millville way. His fiancée was a Miss Reid from Farnley County. She was the reigning belle there, admired and flattered, and it turned her heart to stone to have all the men after her, crazy to marry her. The doctor was a young man then, and he couldn't see any further into her heart, such as it was, than the rest of them.

'She led the doctor a chase before she promised him, they say. But the very day before their marriage was to have taken place, she left her home without a word to anyone to go off with another man who's never been discovered. That broke the doctor up. He took to drugs then, they tell me. The institute had been a big place before — it stood over on Morley's hill; but it burned down one night, and we took this old farmhouse. And the doctor was using the funds, they said, and wasn't responsible at all.

'The trustees found that the money was gone. Nobody knew where it went, because the doctor had his own inheritance, and he wasn't the sort of person to steal or squander. They wouldn't do anything to him because of his family, but they put Mr. Myers in charge of the finances. That's all. None of us liked him, but what could we do about it? He was here when Dr. Jenkins and I were appointed, and as soon as we understood how matters were we agreed to stay as long as we could and try to help the doctor.'

'Mrs. Fraser, I want to know why Mr. Myers incited Dr. Lancaster to use morphine,' said Joan.

'Miss Wentworth — !'

'You know he did. You told me so. And Dr. Jenkins knows.'

The matron looked agitated. 'What

could we do?' she cried. 'Suppose we knew
— what can two people do against a man
like Myers? And suppose we had said something — who would have believed us? We
did all we could do; and we all love the doctor and would rather stay with him and help
where we could than be discharged and do
nothing.' She looked at Joan piteously, like
a child caught in wrongdoing.

'I know you did your best,' answered
Joan. 'But why should Dr. Lancaster stay
here in Myers's power instead of at his
home in Avonmouth, where he's respected
and powerful? Nothing about this matter
is known there.'

The matron wrung her hands. 'I don't
know,' she answered. 'I suppose that man
has had him by the throat in more ways
than we know. Whenever the doctor used
to go to Avonmouth, Mr. Myers would go
with him, and generally he'd come back
with him. Miss Wentworth, till you came
here the doctor wasn't a man; what with
his drugs and the hold Mr. Myers had over
him, he was just a machine. And Mr. Myers
was the driver.'

Joan had the feeling that she should not

listen to the matron's talk about Lancaster; it seemed disloyal of her. But she felt, too, that she *must* know more, and speedily, if she were to thwart that menacing evil which she sensed more and more clearly as the moments passed.

'Aye, but there's worse than that,' continued Mrs. Fraser, dropping her voice. 'I spoke to you of the times when the doctor has come back from Avonmouth, not a man but a devil. I said I'd shoot him then and not think it was the doctor who lay dead before me. Those are the times when Mr. Myers has pulled and pulled until he has pulled the doctor down to his own level. Only two or three times, but the village knows what he is then. That's why the people won't come here when they're ill. Oh, it's pitiful then, Miss Wentworth, and my heart has bled when I've looked into the doctor's face and seen the eyes of a lost soul; my heart has bled in spite of my fears. For he's terrible then, Miss Wentworth — a different man, a wicked man; and I'd rather see the doctor lying dead before me than see him like that. But what am I telling you this for when that hoodoo's gone forever, and, thanks to you, the doctor will never be like that again?'

Joan rose. 'I know that trouble is at an end,' she said. 'And I'm sure Dr. Lancaster is incapable of having misappropriated that money. If Mr. Myers made him think he had done so when he was under the influence of morphine, and has been black-mailing him, that has come to an end also.'

'Yes, Miss Wentworth. And even if doctor did use the money for some purpose or other, he wasn't responsible.'

They went toward the door. Although she was not aware of it, Joan was straining her ears to hear, through the dripping rain, the sound of the buggy wheels. She had been nearly an hour in Mrs. Fraser's room. The sense of imminent danger was growing stronger, but with it was relief that the hour was come. She felt that the revelation was at hand. However terrific that coming battle was to be, at least it would be a blind battle no longer.

The women looked at each other a little uneasily. Each had something to be con-cealed. Presently Mrs. Fraser spoke. 'Dr. Lancaster could never do without you now,

Miss Wentworth,' she said significantly.

Joan hesitated. There was a challenge in the words, but she remembered Lancaster's instructions to her to say nothing about their engagement. She could not act against them.

'Miss Wentworth,' said the matron, placing her hand on the woman's arm firmly, 'there's something else I ought to have told you about. Mrs. Dana — '

'Hark!' interrupted Joan, holding up her hand for silence.

Then they heard, a long distance away and inaudible to one whose attention was not strained, like theirs, the sound of the wheels of Jenkins's buggy.

7

The Demon Reappears

Joan hurried out upon the veranda and stood peering under her raised hand across the rain-swamped fields to where the carriage road wound in and out among the hills. The sun had set and it was beginning to grow dark; a bat was flitting under the eaves, and the steady downpour never ceased. Mrs. Fraser, who had moved to follow her, went back into her room. There was a queer, troubled pucker about her lips, and once she went to the door and looked intently at Joan, who had not stirred from her position of expectancy.

Presently, looking out through the dripping trees, Joan could see the buggy crawling up the hill through the mud. Slowly it moved along the road. Jenkins was driving, and there were two men with him, not one. Joan recognized Lancaster; then she perceived first the hard hat, next

Myers's face under it.

She shuddered. The worst had come about, then. But the last battle was joined, and under her fears she felt a hardening of her spiritual resources. She would not falter. She went slowly toward the top of the three low wooden steps and stood there like a statue, watching the buggy pass up the weed-grown drive until it came to a standstill.

Lancaster and Myers were laughing together, and, as Myers saw Joan, he said something, and Lancaster threw back his head in merriment.

Myers was the first to descend. He raised his hat to Joan and grinned. 'The doctor's come back quite safe, you see,' he said, 'and feeling fine again.'

Joan hardly noticed the man; she was bracing herself to bear what was to come.

Lancaster got out, and Jenkins, contrary to his custom, lashed the horse violently and drove rapidly away. Myers and Lancaster came up the steps of the porch together. Now Lancaster was raising his hat in turn, and under it was the face of the smirking bully of the operating theater at the Avonmouth hospital.

'Well, little runaway, I'm back, you see,' he said with a leer at Joan, and Myers chuckled.

Joan stood aghast, staring at Lancaster. He had the look of a man possessed by a devil, as the matron had said. If this was the man she loved, it was the departed soul she loved, not whatever was animating the body. She could only continue to stare at him, incapable of speech or movement, while Lancaster spoke again.

'Well, I had a fine trip to Avonmouth, my dear, and I hurried back as fast as I could to see you. I couldn't stay away from you very long, Joan, after you saved my life. And I persuaded Mr. Myers to return with me. We're all going to be good friends. Mrs. Fraser! Mrs. Fraser? Where the devil are you?' he bawled.

Mrs. Fraser's frightened face appeared at the door. 'Here, sir!' she stammered.

'Is supper ready? If so, we'll all eat together.'

'It's waiting, sir. I'll lay another place.'

'Good! Then we'll go in. What do you say, Joan, darling? Aren't you glad to see me?' He linked his arm in hers and pulled her toward the door, through which Myers had already preceded them.

But at the door Joan found her voice. She pulled herself away. 'Dr. Lancaster!' she gasped.

'Yes, my dear?'

'What happened? What is it?' she cried wildly.

He bent toward her and kissed her. 'It's the sight of you, little Joan Wentworth,' he said. 'My, you do look a stunner tonight!'

With a sob, Joan tore herself away from him and ran upstairs at the top of her speed. She was choking with grief and shame. Hard as she ran, she knew her flight was an incentive to Lancaster to follow her. He went after her as fast as he could, and as she slammed the door of her room his hand was on the knob outside. She was just too late to turn the key.

'Joan! Joan! Open the door and don't act like a little fool!' he shouted. 'What's the matter with you? Aren't you glad I've come back? Say, I've got a half-dozen bottles of the fizzy stuff in my bag, and we three will make a night of it.'

'Go away!' cried Joan hysterically. 'Leave me alone!'

'The devil!' shouted the doctor, and set shoulder to the door. It crashed open, sending Joan staggering into the center of the room. Lancaster stood before her with an evil, angry, mocking face.

'See here, now,' he began as Joan retreated slowly before him, looking at him in fascinated horror, 'I guess this is a sort of misunderstanding, isn't it, Joan? You haven't turned against me since I left here yesterday? There's none of these spry young farm hands about here has cut me out, eh, dearie?'

'Oh, won't you please leave me?' pleaded Joan. 'Try to remember how — how different you were yesterday.'

'That's true!' he swore. 'I'm different now. I was a sanctimonious mug yesterday. I'm in my right mind today. It gave me the blue creeps, being cooped up here in this godforsaken place. I tell you, Joan, now that I've had enough good liquor to sink that morphine out of my system, I'm feeling like a king. Say, now, come down to supper, and we'll have a great time together. Myers doesn't bear any ill feeling. And we'll put Him out after a while and finish up the bottles ourselves. And say — '

He was advancing toward her with his arms outstretched. Joan sprang back to the washstand and snatched up the half-filled pitcher with such an evident determination to defend herself with it that the man fell back, scowling.

'Joan, don't be a little jackass!' he shouted angrily. 'I know what you mean when you look at me like that. You think you're above being sociable just because I don't choose to stand on my dignity tonight. Did you expect me to go about always looking like a sanctified mummy, as I did when I was ill?'

'Listen, Dr. Lancaster,' panted Joan, 'I'm not going to judge you by what you're saying now. Leave me, and tomorrow, if you are yourself, I shall be willing to hear your explanation, because I know it is not your better self that is speaking. Leave my room now, please, immediately!'

The man glared at her: but he was dominated, in spite of himself, by her courage and apparent calmness.

'Well, I'm not going to fight with you

before I've had my supper,' he answered. 'You think things over, and in a little while I guess you'll see them in a different light. You can't fool me with these mock airs and graces, dearie. I've seen them in women before. Used to believe in them once, too, till I found it meant that it was going to cost me more in the end. You come down and act straight, Joan, see?'

He slammed the door viciously behind him. Joan fell upon her knees beside the bed. There, tearless, but shaken with her grief, she poured out a wild prayer for the lost soul of the man. This was worse than anything she could have divined. Better by far that he had returned as on that earlier day, drugged and possessed by the morphine spirit, than in the chains of this devil. Better that he had died. Even when the shifty, false, lying drug fiend was in control of him, he had never been vicious and vile like this before.

And yet this was the John Lancaster of the Southern Hospital. It was the traditional Lancaster in his hour of relaxation. He treated women shamefully, as the gossiping nurse had said. Joan had never been in fear of physical harm as she was now.

She rose from her knees, looking wildly about her. Then she heard footsteps outside, and she sprang back across the room.

But it was only the matron. Mrs. Fraser cast a scared glance at her and ran forward. 'What did he say to you?' she cried.

'Who is he? What is he?' whispered Joan. 'He's not the John Lancaster I know.'

'Heaven help me if I know what's changed him!' Mrs. Fraser cried. 'This is what I was telling you about this afternoon. Two or three times before, he's come back from Avonmouth like this, acting as if the devil had his soul. What are you going to do?'

'I'm afraid of him. I dare not stay here. Where shall I go?' cried Joan. In the midst of her terror, she suddenly realized that the look upon the matron's face was the same as on her first night, when they had held a brief conversation in the same room.

For a moment Mrs. Fraser did not answer her. The two of them drew together, listening. The men were having supper below, conversing in boisterous tones and laughing loudly. Joan heard her own name spoken, and a renewed outburst of mirth followed.

'Mrs. Fraser,' said Joan, 'the Dr. Lancaster whom I respect and honor is not in that man's body. I'm going away at once. I shall ask Dr. Jenkins to protect me until tomorrow. He's a gentleman; he will do so.'

'You can't go through this storm,' exclaimed the matron, and as she spoke Joan realized that the wind had risen to a hurricane and the boughs creaked and snapped like pistol shots. 'You must stay here tonight. Stay with me and I'll swear he shall not hurt you. Look at this!'

She pulled a revolver from beneath her apron and handed it to Joan.

'I've kept that ever since the last time he came back like this, when he went raving among the patients, mad with liquor. That was the end of the institution. He frightened a sick woman almost to death. Use it on him if you must, because it won't be him you'll kill, but the devil that's got him.' She was almost incoherent with fear.

Joan took the revolver and slipped it into the pocket of her uniform. Oddly enough, she felt that the Lancaster of that evening had so grossly wronged the Lancaster of earlier days that to kill him would be to avenge an intolerable outrage. She hated him with all the intensity of which her heart was capable; hated him for the wrong he had done himself, the outrage on their love. And under the hate, the flame of the love she had borne burned pure and clear.

It was long since dark, but the maid had not lit the lamp outside Mrs. Dana's door, near the head of the stairs. The moon had not yet risen. The women crept cautiously along the hall.

Lancaster and the secretary were in Myers's room. The door was open. Joan heard a cork fly with a bang, and the gurgle of the champagne in glasses. The voices were raised high, and there came the sound of a scuffle.

'Sit down — !' the secretary was crying. 'Do you want to be a fool and spoil everything? Leave her alone until tomorrow.'

'I'm damned if I do!' cried Lancaster.

'Wait a minute. Listen to me. You agreed to come back here and put her out. Why don't you do it now?'

Lancaster laughed coarsely. 'Because

she's too damned pretty, Myers,' he answered.

'It's the drink in you. She isn't any better-looking than any average woman in Avonmouth. See here, now, are you going to bust up the game or are you not?'

'I'll show you!' shouted Lancaster, breaking from Myers's grasp and rushing from the room.

He met the women at the foot of the stairs. His face was flushed, his hair disordered, his manner maniacal. 'You sneak, what are you butting into this show for?' he demanded of Mrs. Fraser.

The matron, cowed by his violence, trembled. She tried to pull Joan toward her room; then caught her eye and made the slightest gesture indicative of shooting. Lancaster raised his fist threateningly.

The matron did not lift a finger to defend herself. She stood quite calmly, awaiting the expected blow. Perhaps it was some atavistic trait inherited through generations of downtrodden ancestors; and yet, servile though it might have been, the look on the woman's face was almost heroic.

The man let his fist fall; he seized the

matron by the shoulders and pushed her back into her room. He turned the key in the lock and put it in his pocket! 'That's settled, I reckon,' he said with satisfaction.

Joan's hand went into her pocket. Her fingers closed about the revolver handle. But at that moment the secretary, who had come out of his room, went up to Lancaster. 'See here, now,' he began to remonstrate, 'have a little sense, Doctor. If you're bent on busting everything up, you and I part company.'

Lancaster turned on him with so menacing a gesture that Myers flung up his hands in despair and went back into his room. Joan stood facing the doctor alone. At that moment her decision was nearly made, and she felt conscious of no fear of him at all. If he attempted violence, she knew what she would do. But he did not lay hands on her. He stood leaning against the newel post at the foot of the stairs, watching her face.

'Joan, I guess you and I are old enough to understand each other,' he said. 'Maybe I've been a bit rough. I was so glad to see you again that I may have let my feelings get the better of me. Now just explain to me, like a sensible woman, what it is that's changed you. Is it because I've come back jolly instead of like a sick man? You were nice enough to me yesterday. You liked me; you know you did. I fired Myers to please you. Now I've brought him back to patch things up, and you shrink from me. What's the matter with you? Do you want Myers to go? Will you act differently if I kick him out right away? Say the word and I'll do it.'

Joan was searching his eyes for the least sign of the man she had known. He broke off, scowling and wincing under her stare. Above his words was the sound of the beating rain, the lashing wind; and from within the matron's room Joan heard Mrs. Fraser crying in prayer: 'Oh, Lord, save her! Save that woman this night, Lord, from the devil! Save her! Save her, Lord!'

'Maybe I got you wrong,' continued the doctor. 'But if I did, I ask you, who's to blame? Didn't you come to me at my house in Avonmouth and ask for your job back? Weren't you as sweet as sugar when you wanted something out of me? And didn't you agree to come up here to work for me? Well, what's the inference, then? You can have your job back if you want it. But I can do better by you than that. You're too pretty for a nurse's job, and I told you so that day you turned on me in the theater like a wildcat. Now, then, it's up to you. Your move, partner!'

'What do you mean by all that?' asked Joan. 'What do you wish me to do?'

He gave her a gratified grin. 'Now you're talking sense, my dear,' he answered. 'Live up to your promise, that's all. A nod's as good as a wink, and you can't fool me with your pretense. I've seen enough women in my life to know that they're all the same. You know why I gave you this job here. Don't try to pretend it was because you're such a clever nurse. I reckon that if I'd wanted a nurse I could have gone no further and found a better one. Live up to your agreement and don't be a little cheat. That's all you've got to do.'

Joan tried to push past him, but he remained at the foot of the stairs, blocking her way.

'Let me pass, please!' she cried. 'I'm going to leave the institute at once.'

'Without your hat?' he sneered.

168

'Let me pass at once!'

'Well, I reckon I can't stop you,' he rejoined. 'Just one word more, though. Do you realize your situation? Do you know what people will say when you go to them with crazy stories about me? Nobody will think you came down here to the notorious John Lancaster after he'd fired you just because you were such a wonderful nurse that he couldn't do without you. What sort of reputation do you expect to have in Avonmouth? You can go, but you won't go there. Not back to Avonmouth, understand that well. I'll hound you out of the town, you little double-crosser!'

For the first time, Joan felt her spirit begin to shrink from the ordeal. She was cowed, almost as helpless as if he had used physical violence toward her. And through the baneful dream she was aware that Myers had come out of his room and was watching the scene from the end of the hall, wearing a smug, complacent smile. Myers was getting his way and having his revenge in one.

And because the situation was too horrible for belief, Joan could remember only the Lancaster of yesterday. She ran to the man and caught him by the arms, and looked into his face with pathetic earnestness. 'I'm going to stay, John!' she cried. 'My faith is stronger than that. I remember what you said to me, and I remember my promise to you. Some day you'll come to yourself and everything will be clear. I shall call to the John Lancaster I know against the man who claims to be him and is not.'

'What do you mean?' shouted the doctor. 'Who do you take me for?'

'You're not the John Lancaster who won my love,' cried Joan with an impassioned gesture. 'Let your better self hear and understand me. You asked me to stay and fight your battle with you, and nothing shall drive me from you till you tell me to go; nothing shall make me falter till I have won you again.'

The man's eyes blazed. 'You're right; you're dead right there, Joan!' he cried, and caught her in his arms. He pressed his lips to hers.

She struggled wildly in his grasp. 'Let me go!' she panted. But she could not free herself. She screamed.

The matron's voice shrieked through the

door. 'Shoot him!' she cried. 'Shoot him dead! Shoot him!'

Joan wrenched her arm free and struck at the man, but he pinioned it. 'I've got you, Joan!' he cried triumphantly. 'And nothing under heaven shall make me let you go.'

Held as she was, Joan got her fingers into her pocket. She thrust the revolver upward into his face. He recoiled with an oath, squinting at the weapon, his face convulsed.

And in that moment, knowledge came to Joan Wentworth. 'You are *not* John Lancaster!' she cried.

As she spoke, they heard the sound of halting footsteps on the porch. The door swung slowly open. Joan's hand dropped to her side, and she slid the revolver mechanically into her pocket. She tried to cry but could not.

Upon the threshold of the door, looking out with a wry, distorted grin on his pale lips, was the man who had held her. And on the threshold looking in, with eyes drug-clouded, swaying and clutching at the door pillars to support himself upright, was the John Lancaster of yesterday. And even Joan, with all her love and hate, could not have told the one man from the other. But with a cry she ran to the Lancaster she knew and caught at him, and felt his arms about her.

It seemed to Joan, long afterward, like some dreadful picture: the swaying man upon the threshold, to whom she clung, and his double within. And then the rasping voice of Myers broke the long silence.

'Well, well,' said the secretary, rubbing his hands together, 'here's a pretty kettle of fish. It will all have to come out now.'

The Lancaster within the door turned his eyes from Joan to Myers; his passion and rage had frozen into malevolence.

'Don't put the blame on me,' said Myers acidly. 'I warned you to get rid of her.'

John Lancaster advanced into the hall. His double, who had drawn back a pace or two, stood watching his efforts to steady himself with a scornful smile. Joan put her hands on her lover's arm; it seemed unbearable that he should display his weakness for them to mock at. But then, glancing into his face, she saw that, weak as he was, and morphine-ridden, too, it was John Lancaster himself, virile in personality and mind, who had come back. Lancaster's double turned fiercely upon the secretary.

'Yes, it's a pretty kettle of fish,' he retorted, 'and it's going to be fried. We'll have this out tonight. Curse you, why didn't you stay here at your post instead of running to me? Were you afraid of this woman?'

'Who is this person?' Joan asked Lancaster.

'My half-brother and my evil spirit,' he answered.

'Why don't you order him to go? Why don't you order them both to go?'

'Because,' replied the other, sneering, 'John Lancaster sold me his birthright for a mess of pottage — morphine pottage. That's why. Because the world knows *me* as John Lancaster, not that outcast who's sunk so low that he sold his very name for drugs.'

'That's a lie,' said Lancaster. 'You stole my name. You devil, you've robbed me of my manhood these four years past.'

'Gentlemen,' cried the secretary, 'we've got to talk this matter over, and this isn't the place. If the agreement has worked any injustice to Dr. Lancaster, no doubt it can be readjusted. It's clear that we've got to come to a sensible understanding. Let's face the facts like men and talk it over in the doctor's room. And the woman had better go upstairs,' he added.

'Miss Wentworth stays with me,' said Lancaster.

The double and the secretary exchanged ironic glances. It was evident that they did not feel themselves to be in the position of trapped conspirators.

'Dr. Lancaster, if you can't order them to leave, is it necessary that you should be drawn into a discussion now?' Joan asked.

'Yes, it's necessary,' said Lancaster. 'I'll fight this thing with Lawson to a finish tonight.'

'Lawson?'

'I believe that I'm Lawson,' said Lancaster's half-brother with a mocking bow.

They went toward Lancaster's room. Joan perceived now that the doctor's weakness was purely a physical one; he dragged his limbs slightly, the curious result of the morphine poisoning that she had noted before.

She went into the room with him,

confident in that belief. Myers closed the door behind them and placed his thickset body in front of it. It was astonishing to see how Lancaster braced himself for the ordeal. He drew himself up, standing erect, and faced the others.

'Dr. Lancaster has the floor,' said Lawson in his sneering voice. 'At least, I understand that the proposal to revise our agreement comes from him.'

'Joan, I owe you an explanation,' said Lancaster, turning toward her. 'This morning, after I operated, I was called to the house which people think is mine — which *should* be mine,' he added with sudden vehemence. 'I was told it was an urgent case. I found these men there. They drew me into an argument, and in the heat of it Myers plunged a needle of morphine into my arm.'

'To quiet you, because you were becoming violent and injuring yourself,' sneered the secretary. 'Yes, I did, and I left you in good hands.'

'They left me senseless in the consulting room, but I managed to force my limbs to obey my will. John Lancaster had still a little more willpower than they counted on. And John Lancaster's name was enough to conjure up a special train this afternoon, though they had robbed me of my money.'

'Your seven dollars was left in the care of the servant,' interposed Lawson. 'Don't be cynical and childish, John. As for the hypodermic that Myers gave you, it was under my instructions, and I accept full responsibility for the action.'

Joan put her hands on Lancaster's shoulders. 'That's all you need to tell me,' she said quietly. 'I knew you'd been trapped by them. I never doubted you.'

Lancaster's eyes blazed. 'No, I'm going to tell you everything,' he answered.

'Better not, John,' said Lawson. 'You'll find it difficult to separate your hallucinations from the substratum of fact which they contain.'

'Oh, let him talk,' said Myers. 'Let's hear the worst he's been storing up against us. Let him get his visions out of his system and maybe he'll feel better.'

'Eight years ago,' said Lancaster, 'I was a man respected in Avonmouth and everywhere throughout the south. Then a domestic trouble overtook me. You know what that was, Joan. It broke me down. I couldn't cope with life. I lost my grip on reality, gave up my work — '

'Yes, John, now we're getting at the truth,' interposed Lawson bitterly. 'You, the honored head of the Southern Hospital, became a common tramp and wandered about the country with hobos, and I've been living down your reputation for you. Go on, John; don't skip the interesting parts.'

'I shall skip nothing. The woman I was to have married left me the evening before, and disappeared with another man. Had he been free to marry her, she would have had no need to escape in secrecy. I gave up my work. I hunted them through the southern states. My mind was obsessed with the idea of redeeming my honor. If I'd found them, I would have killed him. They knew it, and they fled before me. I gave them no rest. For five years I pursued them, running down every clue.'

'You'll permit me to correct your memory on that point, John,' said Lawson suavely. 'For five years you wandered among tramps and hobos, to the scandal of your former friends, thinking that you were looking for your fiancée, but actually doing your searching in morphine visions. Such delusions of phenomenal activity are a recognized symptom of your disease. Our modern-day De Quincey here imagined that he visited every corner of the earth while lying at home in an opium stupor.'

'I never touched morphine until you gave it to me,' said Lancaster.

'That delusion is part of your disease. No, John, you may have searched the suburban districts of Avonmouth, but you can't have gone far, because every few months you'd turn up at the institute, looking shabbier and more disreputable on each occasion, and more and more morphine-soaked. And every time I tried to set you up and help you. I was sorry for you, and you knew it and traded upon my pity. I was shamed by you, and you knew that and traded upon my shame.'

Lancaster hung his head. Joan laid her hand lightly on his, and after that he continued to return Lawson's gaze steadfastly.

'I went to you, Jim Lawson,' he said, 'because I had placed you in charge of the institute when I elected to head the other branch of the trust fund, the Avonmouth Hospital. I gave you the charge here because you were — '

'Your illegitimate half-brother,' said Lawson bluntly. 'We're not mincing our words. Because you robbed me of my own birthright as your elder brother, by reason of the fact that my mother was not legally married to our father. Yes, go on.'

'At last, Joan, I was broken down completely,' continued Lancaster. 'It was a monomania, that search of mine, as I came to understand afterward; a perverted pride that had eaten into my heart and left no place for other thoughts. But I didn't become addicted to morphine until this man urged it upon me, under the guise of medical care. And even then I could have broken off the habit at any time, but I had no heart to, and it gave me relief from thoughts that tortured me.'

'So they *all* think,' said Lawson.

8

The Denunciation

'It was he who told me that I could never break it off,' continued Lancaster; 'who urged me to continue the use of it with sophistical arguments which I had not the energy to oppose. I'd been five years away from Avonmouth. The people at the Southern Hospital believed me dead, and I did not undeceive them. I never meant to return. When I came here, it was always by night, to this man whom I believed to be my friend, to avoid shaming our name in the eyes of Millville. Thus no one ever saw us together, and Lawson and I resembled each other as much as we do today.'

'More, I hope, John,' sneered Lawson. 'The life one leads tells as the years go by.'

'Nobody in these parts had seen me since I was a boy. I left home when I was young and studied at Johns Hopkins and abroad. Lawson had taken my name. The old neighbors had gone away; and if any of the country folk have long memories, they have close tongues, too. The matron and Jenkins are both newcomers. I had passed out of memory.

'This devil saw his chance and grasped at it,' he added with sudden vehemence. 'Here was the famous Dr. Lancaster, a broken man, an outcast, and believed in Avonmouth to be long since dead. And here was the Lancaster known to Millville and Lancaster village, at the head of this institute. Why shouldn't he get me to take his place here while he went to Avonmouth and claimed to be me? Lawson was ambitious. He wanted to be something bigger than the superintendent of a little hill institute. And he wanted to get his fingers on the trust fund at Avonmouth. Do I wrong you?' he demanded, turning fiercely upon Lawson.

'Not in the least; you honor me,' he said with a suave bow. 'I wanted to take the fund out of your worthless supervision and devote it to proper uses.'

'This must be stopped!' shouted Myers with a sudden interposition. 'Dr. Lancaster, you're saying things you'll regret tomorrow.

You're turning to bite the hand that fed you. Where would you be today save for Dr. Lawson? A dead man in a pauper's grave!'

'He persuaded me, weakened as I was by the morphine he'd been dosing me with,' Lancaster resumed, without paying the least attention to the secretary. 'He was to take my place in Avonmouth, while I could assume charge here, pretending to have an illness that would account for any change in my aspect and character. Nobody would know the difference, and nobody has. Here, he told me, I could be free to brood over my unhappy life, while he, the clever schemer, taking up my past, could adapt it to his own. He convinced me.'

Joan gasped as she begun to understand the enormity of the crime. And it was true: she could read it in Lawson's face, his pride in the exploit. Lawson was actually smirking, as he had smirked in the operating theater.

'I consented, and he went away,' said Lancaster. 'My recollection of the months that followed is necessarily a dim one. I know, however, that I was in no state to take care of the funds. They disappeared, and I was accused of having embezzled them. If I did that, I did it in my dreams.'

'That's just the trouble with you, John,' said Lawson. 'You dream too much. The question is, what did you do with them? Bury them? You can't have spent thirty thousand dollars upon morphine.'

'I've accepted and borne the burden of the guilt,' cried Lancaster. 'This man Myers was placed in charge. Thereafter, he was ever at my elbow, urging me upon the downward path. When I would make an effort to break off my habit, he'd whisper to me that my life was ruined; that the charge of embezzlement would be pressed if ever I returned to Avonmouth. He would advise me to take my drug and forget — '

'You're lying, you dreamer!' yelled the secretary. 'You lie, and you know it!'

'When you came, Joan, I was all but hopeless. I caught at your aid as my last hope, because that day you came to me your face looked good — and strong, too; and you spoke so sincerely. It had been years since I'd known anyone like you. You seemed to have been sent to me.'

'Religious hallucination,' said Lawson,

tapping his forehead significantly. Nonetheless, Joan could see that he was growing uneasy as the plot was unraveled.

'It was a miracle, that meeting; one of these chances that seem reserved to uncover such conspiracies. For though this man had stolen my name — ' And here a touch of pride was visible on Lancaster's face. ' — there was one thing he couldn't do. He couldn't perform the Lancaster operation, though he'd picked my brains during the weeks he kept me here, a prisoner in one room.

'And so from time to time he compelled me to go to Avonmouth, under the charge of Myers, in order to operate. He laid down the regulations: I was to dress and mask alone; I was to speak as little as possible and to leave hastily after I had finished my work. And he always sent me there with a full injection of the drug in my body. I was too weak to resist; too much under the thumb of Myers here.'

'Won't you stop this painful recitation of his hallucinations?' pleaded the secretary to Lawson. 'You know, tomorrow he'll retract everything.'

'The day came,' continued Lancaster, ignoring him, 'when a committee of visiting surgeons was to witness the operation. He thought that he'd learned it. His vanity led him to go to the hospital in person after he'd brought me to Avonmouth. The patient died, but he alone was responsible for that. And that's where you come into the case, Joan. I managed to get a word with you, and Myers followed you to this institute in order to forestall me if possible.'

'Dr. Lancaster, you did not steal the funds,' said Joan calmly. 'Don't you see the hold these two men have managed to obtain over you? *They* stole the funds, and their object in drugging you was to get rid of you, the sole evidence of their crime, by your death. And so, not daring to murder you, they planned that you should commit suicide.'

'You'll answer for that!' shouted the secretary, white with rage.

Lancaster shrugged his shoulders. 'It doesn't matter now, my dear,' he said.

But he had struck Lawson through his triple hide of vanity at last. 'But that isn't all,' shouted the man. 'Admit that there may be a substratum of truth in these morphine dreams of yours, John Lancaster. Admit that I was ambitious, and that I did take the place my half-brother had forfeited in order to be of use to the world, and in order to save you from a felon's cell or a maniac's grave. Acknowledge that I did impersonate you tonight, as before, and that I came back with Myers in order to get rid of this woman who threatened to disrupt the institute and put a drug fiend in the office I hold. Well, what then? That isn't all the story.

'You've played your miserable game craftily, John Lancaster, after having made a fair agreement with me. But I've done my duty toward you and your father's fund, and if he were alive he'd thank me for it. And as for this woman, she can go; and if her ravings receive credence anywhere, I'll face a jury and tell the truth fearlessly.

'But you haven't explained everything to your poor dupe, John. You haven't told her where your sweetheart is. You haven't said that all the while you've been making love to her, your fiancée is under this roof, hopelessly insane; that she came back in her madness, and that you took her into the institute and cared for her when her own people had discarded her, because you still loved her. And I'll tell you something, John. I brought her back. I was in touch with her from first to last, and I brought her here as an additional lure to keep you at the institute after I'd gone to Avonmouth. Just tell Miss Wentworth who Mrs. Dana is.'

Joan's eyes met Lancaster's, and she saw in his the supreme moment of his anguish. She braced herself to meet the shock; she told herself that Lancaster no longer cared for his poor charge. She faced Lawson and Myers unflinchingly. But the spring of hope that had been bubbling in her heart seemed to have gone dry.

Lawson seemed to be animated by some infernal devilry, throwing off the mask he had assumed. He leaned forward and shook his finger in Lancaster's face. 'And there's another thing, John,' he said. 'You remember that when we were boys together, I resented the difference between your position and mine. Because of a few written words upon a legal document, you, the younger, were the honored heir of John Lancaster senior, living in the big house on the estate, while I was the unacknowledged child, the shame of my poor mother, ostracized by the whole district. Your friends pretended not to know who I was when they rode by.'

Lancaster made a gesture of deprecation as Lawson's voice shook with passion. 'That's true, Jim,' he said. 'But can you blame me? Did I not give you the position here?'

'I hated you because of that, John,' resumed Lawson. 'I wanted to be a surgeon. What a struggle I had, working my way through Johns Hopkins while you were spending your father's money there! The struggle soured me. And once, do you remember, I was operating on a rabbit under curare, which had paralyzed the motor nerves and left the beast to suffer? It was an experiment such as I had often thought I should like to make on you, and you flung a vile word at me and killed the creature. I told you then that I would get even with you some day. Well, the time arrived. I got my own back, and more. But there's one thing I never told you. Your fiancée was the victim of a misunderstanding. There was no other man.'

John Lancaster's deep breathing seemed the only sound in the room. As if galvanized into full strength, he stood now like a panther poised for a leap, every muscle grown taut, his eyes gleaming. Joan, paralyzed by the sudden unleashing of Lawson's venomous revenge, could not utter a word.

Lancaster spoke: 'You said you were in touch with her and brought her here after she became insane. How did you do it?'

'You've had your full say, John Lancaster,' replied Lawson, 'and now I'm going to have mine. Under the delusion that your intention was to elope with her, on the day before the one that was fixed for the marriage in the parish church — a romantic plan to evade the family and curious neighbors — Miss Reid went to Savannah, to meet you there. I needn't go into the details of the trap that your unacknowledged enemy set for you; but when she learned she'd been tricked, it was too late to return. Her life was ruined, John — and it was *I*, impersonating *you*, who sent her there.'

Without a sound, Lancaster leaped at him. Joan saw the secretary snatch up the lamp and hold it on high. She heard his screaming, terrified voice above the uproar. He stood like some squat statue illuminating the space above the dark in which Lancaster and Lawson sprawled, clutching at each other like two primeval cave men. It was grotesque, for it was like a man fighting with himself; and, in fact, it might have been Lancaster fighting with his evil angel. He was no match for Lawson, but at first his pent-up fury, at last unleashed, matched the two equally.

Then Lawson flung his adversary from him and struggled to his knees. As Lancaster grasped him and tried to rise, he flung him down again. Lancaster's head struck the corner of the iron bedstead. His hands unclosed; he sighed and lay perfectly still. Joan saw the look of malignant rage upon Lawson's face; saw him raise his heel above the face of the unconscious man. He would have ground out Lancaster's life, but that Joan pulled the revolver from her pocket and thrust it into his face for the second time.

Lawson staggered backward, rage and terror depicted upon his features in the light

of the swaying oil lamp. At that moment
Myers was crouching near her. He set the
lamp down. Joan felt a sharp pain in the
upper part of her arm. She saw the secretary putting something into his pocket. He
dodged the wavering revolver and backed
toward the door, pulling Lawson with him.

'I'm going to finish this!' yelled Lawson.

9

Hope and Light

Myers clutched at him and pulled him into the hall. Joan heard the secretary's eager whispers as Lawson's struggles and angry mutterings gradually subsided. Then she heard them enter Myers's room, and, forgetting them instantly, she bent over Lancaster and raised his head upon her knee.

He was breathing heavily. The blow had only stunned him. Joan tried to lift him onto the bed, but he was too heavy for her. As she was attempting to do so, however, the door opened and Mrs. Fraser came in.

'I found a key,' she whispered, trembling. 'I heard them fighting. Heaven help me, what has that devil done to the doctor?'

'He isn't badly hurt,' said Joan. 'Help me get him on the bed.'

Mrs. Fraser and Joan succeeded. Lancaster lay there, still unconscious. The matron clung heavily to the bedstead, looking at Joan piteously. 'I know it all now,' she muttered. 'I would have known before if I'd listened to the Millville gossip. That devil is his brother.'

'Yes,' said Joan shortly. 'What are you going to do, Mrs. Fraser?'

'I'm going to stand by the doctor,' the woman answered. 'I stood by him year after year when I thought he was possessed by an evil spirit. Why wouldn't I stand by him now?'

'Good,' said Joan. 'And I, too. Tomorrow we'll make short work of these men.'

'Heavens! You — you don't know that man, Miss Wentworth. He's a devil. He has no pity. And his companion is a devil ten times worse than himself.'

'Myers? Who is he?'

'He was his assistant here. He was tried once, they tell me, for poisoning his sweetheart. He sent her candy — but they couldn't find any poison in her body. It was his master who made the analysis, and he lied to get Myers free and have his hold on him. It's all plain to me now, Miss Wentworth.'

'If you knew this,' said Joan, 'you should

have told me. You should have told the police — told anyone rather than let him drug Dr. Lancaster day after day.'

'I thought it was the doctor who was in league with him,' the matron muttered. 'Miss Wentworth, I'm timid and easily frightened, but not another day will I keep silent. Tomorrow ... '

'Yes, tomorrow,' said Joan. 'You'd better go to bed now, Mrs. Fraser. I'll guard the doctor with my revolver, and tomorrow we'll end these years of slavery. Dr. Lancaster is a free man. The past is all behind us.'

The matron slipped away stealthily to her room. Joan took her seat beside Lancaster, listening to the incoherent mutterings which had begun. Presently his eyes opened. He stared at her for some minutes until recognition came into them.

'Joan!' he whispered, stretching out his hand to hers.

She let him take and hold it, and sat beside him while he began muttering again. Gradually he began to realize where he was and to remember.

'It is all true, then, Joan,' he said. 'He's

had his revenge for his fancied wrongs. He's had the best years of my life, and he's beaten me in the end.'

'Beaten you?' echoed Joan. 'You are not beaten. They're at their wits' end what to do now, and tomorrow you'll send them packing and begin your new life.'

'A pitiful hope,' he answered. 'He has given me back one thing — my faith in that poor woman upstairs, and with it a greater faith in humanity; but he's robbed me of all my hope.'

'Why, John?'

'Because I could not have imagined that humanity was so vile. Joan, I'm crushed by his revelation. If he entered this room now, I feel that his will would dominate mine.'

'Those are the words of a sick man,' said Joan. 'Tomorrow you'll be strong. Why, hardly a man on earth could do what you've done with the morphine.'

'I suppose I shall carry on my fight,' he answered wearily. 'But victory will mean nothing to me.'

'I shall stand by your side until I've seen you conquer, and until I've seen you happy in your success.'

'And then, Joan?'

'Then? I shall go away somewhere, I suppose.'

'Go away? From me? Is it because of Mrs. Dana?'

'Because of her, John.'

'But she's nothing to me. She was never anything. Even my monomania of revenge rose out of wounded pride, not love. Surely you won't leave me because I once thought I loved another?'

'It isn't that, John. But, you see, she's been an integral part of your life all these years. Even though her mind was gone, the consciousness of her presence ate into your brain; she was the mainspring of your existence here. She would have been your wife today but for your half-brother's scheme. She's innocent, she has been deeply wronged, and her life has become bound up with yours indissolubly. There's no getting away from that.'

'But don't you know she hates me? She thinks that my death will avenge her wrongs and cure her of her troubles. She's tried three times to kill me. In some mysterious manner she's learned the location of my room. Once she stabbed me in the wrist with a table knife. Once she got the matron's revolver, but fortunately it was unloaded. I've been planning to send her somewhere where she could be better cared for and where my presence would not be a constant incitation to her.'

Joan shook her head. 'It's all part of the past,' she said. 'One can't erase the past. You know that, John.'

'Then you don't love me, Joan?'

She turned her face away; the tears that filled her eyes came from the depths of her being. Lancaster took both her hands in his.

'Do you love me, Joan?'

'Too well to wrong you and myself.'

He drew her toward him, and she remained with her cheek resting against his and his arms about her. She could not stir. A strange physical lethargy seemed to hold her limbs, but her will was unshaken.

'Your last word, Joan?' whispered Lancaster.

'No, dear,' she answered.

The humorous look that came at such odd moments into Lancaster's eyes flickered there now. 'Your very last?' he asked.

'Oh, don't ask me to deny my resolution,' she said.

She released herself and stood beside him. As she did so, she had a sensation as if her feet were resting on a cushion of air. Her physical weakness was matched by her sense of instability; she longed with all her heart to lean within the arms outstretched toward her. She knew that if she had given Lancaster life, he could give her the strength of life; he was of her own people, and all that was chivalric and dear in the land she had loved seemed embodied in him. And before her she saw the closing hospital walls of some far distant city. She must exile herself from everything that she had known.

'You stubborn little thing, Joan!' said Lancaster tenderly. 'But I shall go on loving you.'

'And I love you, John.'

'I shall hear from you sometimes?'

'Yes. And I'll remain in Avonmouth until your battle is won. But there will be no battle. They know that they're beaten. You'll never be weak again.'

'No. But, Joan, if you'd said yes to me, it

would have been so easy.'

She stooped and kissed his forehead. 'You must try to sleep now,' she said. 'I'll leave the revolver with you, and you must lock your door.'

'I'm not afraid of them,' he answered. 'They can do nothing. Keep the revolver for your own safety.'

That seemed the better way. There was nothing that the pair could do to Lancaster. If they targeted anyone, it would be Joan. She understood, and went out without speaking to Lancaster again.

In the hall she breathed more freely. It was ended now, and she knew that she had done the right thing; the only possible thing. But Lancaster had not surmised the terrific battle she had fought during those last few minutes. She did not mean to sleep, but to be awake with her door open, resting and listening for any movements in the house. But though her brain was awake, she was more tired than she had ever been in her life. She could hardly drag her limbs upstairs, and again she had that sense of walking on air.

Under the little burning lamp, she

stopped again to gather strength to go to her room. The ticking of the clock in the hall below was the only sound in the house. She strained her ears to catch the sound of voices from Myers's room, but she could hear nothing. Yet the men could not be asleep. They must be planning together.

The silence in the ramshackle old building was a ghastly one. It seemed to hide innumerable thoughts, as if those of all who had ever lived within its walls survived, breaking upon her brain in invisible waves. She felt enmeshed in a web, as the dreamer who struggles to wake into free life from the horrors of a nightmare. The wind had gone down and the raindrops dripped rhythmically from the eaves.

10

Conclusion

Joan had an intense inclination to surrender; to run back into Lancaster's room, and cry to him to help her and let her fight beside him as long as he lived. And the silence, which was becoming more terrific every moment, was unmistakably malevolent.

She reached her room and tried to shake away her fears. She went to the window and leaned out. The night was clearing and a delicious air blew in from the hills. Not a light was to be seen in Millville or Lancaster. And she wept again, heart-broken. It was all ended, that peace which had begun to enclose her, and all her hopes and all that love which was bound up so intimately with the idea of home.

She lit her lamp, but her fingers slipped over the glass, and it fell to the floor with a crash that startled all the echoes in the old building. The smoky wick flared up.

Joan turned it down with difficulty until the blaze was extinguished, and staggered to the bed, amazed at her weakness.

She could not keep her eyelids open, and she let them close wearily. But sleep was far from her, and still she listened. And after a while an unmistakable sound reached her.

Somewhere within the institute she heard a key turn in a lock. It was the slightest distant sound, but cut the darkness like a knife. And to her mind the sound, which might mean nothing — might be, indeed, the key of Lancaster's door — seemed like the snap of a trap.

She slept and could not awaken. Or, rather, she did not sleep; could not have slept. Yet sleep had paralyzed her limbs and left her brain untouched; and her mind seemed preternaturally acute, so that she felt and saw everything that was happening in the building.

Someone was coming along the passage, as on that night before. The hand was upon the door. Through her closed and paralyzed eyelids, Joan yet seemed to see the figure of the madwoman. Something was in her hand. It was the revolver which Joan had left upon the little table beside her.

Mrs. Dana stood over her, the weapon aimed at her, while her eyes sought her face.

Was she dreaming? Joan waited through an agony of centuries, and the woman was gone. Once more there was silence everywhere. And still she lay there helpless, feeling all and knowing all, and that it had been no dream, but the prelude of worse to come.

It was strange, but she did not once picture Lancaster as being in danger. It was as if the unchained spirit of evil, impotent to harm him, sought another victim. She waited, it seemed, for eons. And then the blow fell.

She heard a man's scream of fear, dinned through her ears distantly, with the accompanying pistol shot. Yet she was unable to stir, and it passed into her memory as of something infinitely long ago. Presently there came the hum of voices chattering cries; bare feet that ran wildly along the corridor without; hands at her door.

It was Mrs. Fraser's voice. Now, with a mighty effort, Joan shook herself free from the spell. She staggered from the bed and groped her way across the room.

Nobody was at the door now, but when she unlocked it a whirl of smoke burst in. It filled the passage. On the floor beneath, a woman was screaming. There were voices outside and the sound of men running along the passages, but Joan could not locate them.

She staggered through the smoke, feeling for the stairs. The haze blinded her. She fell against a wall, felt a rigid body before her, and perceived dimly Mrs. Dana's face wearing a look of exaltation.

She had come too far; she had reached the door of Mrs. Dana's room. Through a break in the smoke cloud, Joan saw that the door was closed. Behind it someone was hammering. Then Myers's screams broke through the din and confusion. He was battering against the door, but, built to resist such pressure, it refused to yield. His cries were terrifying. Under the door came little creeping tongues of flame.

Joan caught at Mrs. Dana. 'Come with me!' she mumbled. 'Come!'

The woman stood rigid as a statue. She felt like marble to the touch, but there was the same exaltation upon her face.

'Open the door!' whispered Joan with her last strength, and pointed. 'Open it! Somebody is locked inside.'

Myers was yelling as Joan had once heard a horse yell that was trapped in a burning stable. The wood of the door was smoldering.

Joan tried to reach the key. But the rigid body barred her way. Then she heard her name called through the smoke. At the cry, Mrs. Dana snatched the key from the lock and began to run along the corridor. Joan saw her dimly through the enwrapping haze. She staggered and fell into Lancaster's arms.

That was her last effort. Incapable of speech, she felt him bear her along the passage, where the smoke clouds were now shot with streaks of flame. They thickened about her. Lancaster was carrying her down the stairs now, while hungry flames sprang at them from the walls and floor. He was staggering drunkenly when they reached the hall below.

He placed her on the grass and plunged back into the flames. The institute was ablaze; fire streamed from the roof and windows. A group of villagers clustered upon the lawn looked on helplessly. Joan saw Jenkins, leading the matron, approaching her. Behind them was Lucy the maid. She tried to tell him that Lancaster had gone back; she could not speak, but he understood her look.

'The doctor's safe,' he said, and as he spoke Joan saw Lancaster among a group of men who had gathered about something wrapped in a blanket.

He rose and came to her. That was all Joan remembered.

And for days and nights her memories of the past were cut short with Lancaster's return that night, borne back by the power of her love flung forth across the miles between them. She knew that he lived; and as the nightmare of the end filtered into her mind, there came with it the sense of an abiding peace, as if the past was dead with all its terrors.

Sometimes she felt that Lancaster was beside her, but when at last complete consciousness returned Joan found herself in bed in a strange house. Through the windows she could see the outlines of the familiar mountains gilded in the red sunset glow against the blue of the sky. Beside her sat a figure which seemed to be so remotely of the past that it was difficult to refrain from laughing at the incongruity of the sight.

It was Jenkins. As Joan stirred, he turned toward her.

'The doctor didn't steal that money,' murmured Joan weakly.

Jenkins laughed as if her words amused him immensely. 'Why, Miss Wentworth, you've been saying that to me every time you woke these five days past, but I couldn't ever get you to tell me how you knew it.'

'I don't remember saying it before,' said Joan.

'I reckon you've been pretty weak. But tell me how you know it.'

'I just know that Dr. Lancaster wouldn't steal anything. Where is he?'

'I'll fetch him, Miss Wentworth. He wants to see you; he's been sitting beside you for days waiting till you really woke up.'

'I'm not burned?' she asked in alarm.

'Not the least little bit. I'll bring you a mirror.'

'No, I'll take you on trust. What made me ill?'

The doctor hesitated. The old obstinate look began to close down on his features. But Joan caught him by the arm ingratiatingly. 'Come, now, tell me,' she said. 'Did he inject morphine into me?'

'No,' said Jenkins, unable to hold out. 'It wasn't morphine. It was curare — the stuff that paralyzes the motor nerves without destroying consciousness.' His face grew somber. 'It doesn't leave traces as morphine does, and that devil had put it into morphine bottles and made the doctor think he was a morphine fiend. They hoped to kill him more quickly, but somehow he got used to it, and I guess they were at their wits' end when you came along. But I'll call the doctor, Miss Wentworth.'

When he was gone Joan lay back on her pillows, looking out into the mountains. She knew what had occurred that night; in her drugged state she had seen the whole dreadful picture — Myers unlocking Mrs. Dana's door and leading her to Joan's room, where she had obtained the revolver; her journey to Lancaster's room, bent on her dreadful mission; the murder of Lawson in the room opposite instead, for reasons which would never be known but were certainly providential.

She saw further by the same intuition, which told her that it had been Mrs. Dana's body wrapped in the blanket upon the lawn. Myers, knowing Joan to be drugged and believing Lancaster dead, had waited in Dana's room and given her the matches on her return with which to start the fire, hoping thus to make sure of his victims and cover up his tracks. And he had fallen into the trap he had baited. Strong as he was, there must have been a stronger power fighting him with Mrs. Dana's arms that night when she turned the key in the lock and left him to die as he had willed Joan to.

But Joan knew that no word of this would ever pass between Lancaster and her. And, indeed, as she lay back and looked across the fields toward the mountains, she felt that something had turned that page, so that it had become not only of the dead past, but unreal in a way, and only the present peace existed.

She heard a quick step without. Lancaster

stood in the doorway, came toward her, knelt at her side, and took her hands in his. And with that, even the memories of the past became tenuous, half-forgotten.

'Dear, it has come true,' he said tenderly.

She lay happily in his arms, looking out all the time toward the sunset on the hills. There was so little to say, because their lives were only beginning.

'I don't want to go back to Avonmouth,' she said at length.

'Nor I, Joan. This is our country.'

'It must always be our country. But — but the fight, John?'

'I'm way ahead of you, my dear,' he answered gaily. 'I fought my fight while you were ill. I've resigned from the hospital — nobody guesses anything there — and I've convinced the trustees here, by my appearance, and by the presentation of certain papers happily discovered after the fire, that I'm a responsible, moral person, honest enough to head the new institute which we are going to build — guess where!'

She looked at him. Then: 'That village in the mountains,' she cried happily. 'Where our lives *really* began. I couldn't wish for anything better.'

'And the patient is going to be our porter. And Dr. Jenkins will be the house surgeon, resident with his wife — Joan, he didn't tell you about Mrs. Fraser? Jenkins! *Jenkins!*' His voice rang through the little house. 'Come in at once and face the fire like a man instead of slinking away into your consulting room, you ruffianly young benedict!'

We do hope that you have enjoyed reading this large print book.

Did you know that all of our titles are available for purchase?

We publish a wide range of high quality large print books including:
Romances, Mysteries, Classics
General Fiction
Non Fiction and Westerns

Special interest titles available in large print are:
The Little Oxford Dictionary
Music Book, Song Book
Hymn Book, Service Book

Also available from us courtesy of Oxford University Press:
Young Readers' Dictionary
(large print edition)
Young Readers' Thesaurus
(large print edition)

For further information or a free brochure, please contact us at:
Ulverscroft Large Print Books Ltd.,
The Green, Bradgate Road, Anstey,
Leicester, LE7 7FU, England.
Tel: (00 44) **0116 236 4325**
Fax: (00 44) **0116 234 0205**

FURY DRIVES BY NIGHT

Denis Hughes

Captain Guy Conway of the British Secret Intelligence sets out to investigate Fortune Cay, a three-hundred-year-old cottage on the Yorkshire coast. The current owner is being terrorised by his new neighbour, who Guy fears could be his arch-nemesis, an international mercenary and war criminal whom he thought he had killed towards the end of the Second World War. En route to the cottage, Conway rescues an unconscious woman from her crashed car — only to find that their lives are inextricably linked as they fight to cheat death . . .

JESSICA'S DEATH

Tony Gleeson

Detectives Jilly Garvey and Dan Lee are no strangers to violent death. Nevertheless, the brutal killing of an affluent woman, whose body is found in a decaying urban neighborhood miles from her home, impacts them deeply. Their investigative abilities are stretched to the limit as clues don't add up and none of the possible suspects seem quite right. As they dig deeper into the background of the victim, a portrait emerges of a profoundly troubled woman. Will they find the answers they need to bring a vicious killer to justice?

WHITE WIG

Gerald Verner

A passenger is found shot dead in his seat on a London bus when it reaches its terminus. Apart from the driver and conductor, there have only been two other passengers on the bus, a white-haired man and a masculine-looking woman, who both alighted separately at earlier stops. To the investigating police, the conductor is the obvious suspect, and he is held and charged. The man's fiancée hires private detective Paul Rivington to prove his innocence — and it turns out to be his most extraordinary and dangerous case to date . . .

THE GHOST SQUAD

Gerald Verner

Mingling with the denizens of the underworld, taking their lives in their hands, and unknown even to their comrades at Scotland Yard, are the members of the Ghost Squad — an extra-legal organization answerable to one man only. The first Ghost operative detailed to discover the identity of the mastermind behind the buying and selling of official secrets is himself unmasked — and killed before he can report his findings to the squad. Detective-Inspector John Slade is his successor — but can he survive as he follows a tangled trail of treachery and murder?

THE MISSING ATTORNEY

Mary Wickizer Burgess

The lone survivor of a car accident during a winter snowstorm, Hal Watson is left stranded far from home. He has just witnessed the gruesome murder of his daughter, Marilyn — but will he be rescued in time to prevent a miscarriage of justice? Attorney Gail Brevard and her colleagues are dismayed when Marilyn's fiance, Damon Powell, is accused of the crime. Gail had successfully defended Damon when he was charged with murder five years earlier. Is this a copycat killing, or is there a serial killer on the loose?

DEATH DIMENSION

Denis Hughes

When airline pilot Robert Varden's plane is wrecked in a thunderstorm, he goes to bail out. As he claws his way through the escape hatch, he is struck by lightning and his consciousness fades into oblivion. Miraculously, Varden cheats death, and awakes in hospital after doctors succeed in saving his life. But he emerges into an unfamiliar world that is on the brink of devastating war, and where his friends are mysteriously seventeen years older than he remembered them . . .